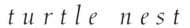

t u r t l e   n e s t

Chandani Lokugé migrated to Australia from Sri Lanka. Her first novel, *If the moon smiled,* was published by Penguin in 2000. It was shortlisted for the NSW Premier's Literary Award – Best novel in 2001, and also for the Community Relations Commision Award 2001. Chandani is the author of the collection *Moth and Other Stories* published in 1994 and her short fiction has been widely anthologised.

Chandani lives in Melbourne. She is a lecturer in English, and Director, Centre for Postcolonial Writing at Monash University.

Also by Chandani Lokugé

Moth and Other Stories
If the moon smiled

CHANDANI LOKUGÉ

turtle nest

PENGUIN BOOKS

Penguin Books

Published by the Penguin Group
Penguin Books Australia Ltd
250 Camberwell Road, Camberwell, Victoria 3124, Australia
Penguin Books Ltd
80 Strand, London WC2R 0RL, England
Penguin Putnam Inc.
375 Hudson Street, New York, New York 10014, USA
Penguin Books, a division of Pearson Canada
10 Alcorn Avenue, Toronto, Ontario, Canada M4V 3B2
Penguin Books (NZ) Ltd
Cnr Rosedale and Airborne Roads, Albany, Auckland, New Zealand
Penguin Books (South Africa) (Pty) Ltd
24 Sturdee Avenue, Rosebank, Johannesburg 2196, South Africa
Penguin Books India (P) Ltd
11, Community Centre, Panchsheel Park, New Delhi 110 017, India

First published by Penguin Books Australia 2003

10 9 8 7 6 5 4 3 2 1

Cover and text design by Nikki Townsend, Penguin Design Studio
Author photograph by Private Collections Photography
Cover images © Getty Images
Typeset in Sabon by Midland Typesetters, Maryborough, Victoria
Printed and bound in Australia by McPherson's Printing Group, Maryborough, Victoria

National Library of Australia
Cataloguing-in-Publication data:

    Lokugé, Chandani.
    Turtle nest.

    ISBN 0 14 029916 5.

    I. Title
    A823.3

This project has been assisted by the Commonwealth Government through the Australia
Council, its arts funding and advisory body.

www.penguin.com.au

For Mala

. . . far out, among the rocks of Lihiniya Island, dozens of baby turtles hatch under sand, and crawl out. They search blindly, and scramble to the silver sea. The eagle swoops. In mid-air the infant splays its limbs and reaches trustingly into the shell-crushing talons.

On the mainland, a woman rests against a coconut tree, her arm raised and circled around it. She sees, in silhouette, the eagle on the craggy ledge, dismembering its prey. She bends over and into herself.

Day is born: a marigold sky.

p a r t   o n e

'Are you Priya?' Aruni asks.

But it is only Simon sitting in the old rattan chair. He looks up startled. The girl seemed to have appeared from nowhere, flung onto the beach like a coconut desultorily husked by the sea. In the half-light of daybreak, his world is foggy, shadow edged. He wipes his eyes and fumbles for his spectacles lying on the sand. She bends down, grabs the spectacles and hands them to him.

Simon squints up into her face through the lenses that she has carelessly touched and blurred. He wipes them on his towel, and sees her more clearly now. He frowns, stretches out his hand as if to touch a dream. But there are only voices.

– See, Mala, the sunrise.

– Simon aiye, let's go closer so we can touch the sun.

His face softens as to the urge of a cherished song. 'I'm sorry,' he mumbles at last. 'What did you want, missy?'

'I am here to meet someone called Priya. I thought it was you.' Her voice rasps like sand on glass. They'd misled her back at the hotel. She stands purposeless.

Hearing her voice, Simon is again distracted. Far out on the beach, someone is running towards him, a waif, a shadow hiding from the lightening dawn. He listens like a man whose vision is failing, listens for the voice that the wind chases towards him.

– Look, Simon aiye, the turtles.

Entranced even now, by its lilt, its richness, he reaches out. And bends towards small arms tugging at him from the infinite past. He scoops her up, and she wriggles and buries her face in his neck.

– Take me to the sea, take me to the sea!

She twists in his arms, leaning towards the waves, her little feet pushing against his body. Laughing, he turns to do as she wills . . .

Simon leans back in his chair and closes his eyes. But the rising sun pierces red and relentless. 'No, I am Simon,' he says. 'A family friend.'

Aruni blinks rapidly. She knows nothing of this place. But she looks around, as if she too can feel the shadow shapes and hear their voices. She shivers, and wraps her beach cloth around her thin body. She wants to zoom in at once, to the very core of it. But it is all so difficult. People, always so secretive, holding back. Clinging to their memories, barring her from entering, as if it were their story alone. But it is *her* story, hers more than anyone else's.

'So where is this Priya? Where can I find him?' she demands, her eyes running up and down the beach.

Simon gets out of his chair then, adjusts his sarong respectfully, and rearranges the towel on his shoulders. He looks at her and uneasily looks away. Young girl with suffering face . . . Desolate and confused, the eyes of the broken-winged bird that Priya held in his palm. It hid in corners under Simon's bed on the verandah. One day it flew away still angry and without a backward glance.

There is something familiar about her. He knows he's known her. 'Here, sit down in this chair for a minute. Would you like me to cut open a kurumba for you, missy?' he asks deferentially, lifting a large green coconut off the heap. And then, taking a machete to cut it, he asks reluctantly, 'Who are you, missy?'

'My name is Aruni Ratnayake. My real mother's name is Nirmala. I have come looking for her. From Australia.' The words struggle out like constricted sobs.

She adds, 'My middle name is Kumari . . . I was named after a dead sister.' Almost an afterthought, grudgingly acknowledged. Dredged from the murky past.

But all movement has stilled. Simon's arm remains raised, the machete poised. 'Kumari,' he murmurs, 'her middle name is Kumari.' The air is translucent, patterns struggling to form – edges of shapes seeking the edges of others. From long ago, Simon hears Priya's whisper in his ear, feels Priya's breath on his face.

– And Mala akka said if the baby is a girl, she'd call her Kumari, after the dead child in the Corner House.

Curious, the heads that push out of hard safe shells. He wants to thrust them back, so they can lie inviolate. He strikes the coconut with the machete, cuts it around the stalk and slices the top.

'Priya is my uncle, my *real* mother's younger brother.'

My uncle, she says, my mother's brother. He feels that she is claiming something that has belonged to him all this time, to him and Priya.

She thrusts her hand in her backpack. She pulls out the precious envelope, worn with handling, and removes the serrated-edged, black and white photograph. Simon hesitates even to touch it. He offers her the cut coconut instead. But she refuses it. He burrows it in the sand. And then, wiping his hands on his towel, he takes the photograph and peers into it. He draws his finger on the faded picture, along the girl's face and body. Priya, a boy then, stands in her shadow, straining to reach at least up to her shoulder, thin and hungry.

'That's my *real* mother with her brother Priya. Do you recognise them?' she asks in her grating voice. She takes a step closer to him. At once, moving away from her, he returns the photograph.

'Yes,' he commits reluctantly, craving solitude. She wants to gut them out, he thinks, without a care for the blood and pain that would spill. He looks back towards his house, the wooden bed on the verandah.

But Aruni's face is suffused by the sunrise – warm and orange. She knows the search is over; she's closer to home than she's ever been.

'You knew her then, you knew my real mother?' She requires confirmation, outstaring him with her intense eyes.

'Yes,' he repeats finally, 'I knew her. I knew them all . . . We used to call her Mala.' His voice is low; he speaks more to himself than to her. She moves closer, wary but yearning – connects with nothing.

'So where is Priya? Tell me, I have to know.'

Simon is moved by her persistence. 'Missy, he lives further down the beach. Over that way. You can meet him when he comes out of his house. Maybe a bit later.'

She looks at where he points, at the fishing village. She looks and looks, as if one house would be marked out for her with a red cross or a flag or something. But they are all the same, huddling in a wavering line between railroad and beach. Here and there, a wooden slat is pushed open. A woman stands at a barred window combing down her hair. A child emerges and runs down to the sea. A dog follows, nose to the sand.

Her mother had lived in one of those huts. She had walked on this very beach. She had given birth to her somewhere in this area. It is all too much to take in. Suddenly Aruni does not know what to do. She hovers in the unknown – should she rush into the village, or back to the hotel? And back to Australia? She looks away from the village. The hotel nestles in lush green. She does not know what to do.

'Priya must be asleep still. You can meet him a little later when he comes this way.' Simon notices her wavering expressions, her clenched fists. He touches the edges of her mood with a kind of tenderness. He offers her the kurumba once again. 'Here, drink some of this – the water is honey sweet.'

And then, choosing his words carefully, he tells her: 'You know, missy, I even knew the gentleman and lady who adopted you. You all lived in the Corner House, not too far away from here, didn't you? I remember you were just about eight years old when you all went to live in Australia – and that must be about ten years ago. How are they? Your parents? Are they well? Are they with you here?'

'No, they are back in Melbourne. I came alone. My father told me where I had to come.' Father . . . my father. His voice, echoing in empty spaces.

Beautiful and useless, his love. She had to leave him behind.

'She's dead. I know my real mother's dead, and everyone else in the family except her brother. But I have to know about her, see?'

Plaintively, she takes the coconut from Simon and lifts it to her lips. He offers a paper straw but she wants to drink like a local. She gulps the water rushing down at too acute an angle. It floods down all over her. Suddenly overcome, she throws the coconut aside, and bends to wipe her wet face on her cloth. The remaining water flows out of the nut and makes a dark patch on the sand. Simon's eyes linger on it.

He sinks back into his chair, tired by the intrusions. Aruni stares down at him, resenting his exclusion of her. She waits but he does not respond. She walks towards the sea. The sun is too bright, the sky blue as blue. A boy waves as he jogs along leaving behind a trail of footprints. 'Morning, missy,' he shouts. She tries to smile, and waves back. But he does not pause. She watches him until he is way past the village, a speck on the endless beach.

The waves spread lacy white fronds at her feet. She bends down, scoops a handful of froth. Tiny rainbows shimmer in her palm. She breathes in the warming air. She presses her palms to her breasts to curb the rush of hope. She'd cup the moment and lock it in her heart if only she knew how. But it expands and tightens and hurts, and she must stretch out her arms and release it. These my people, she thinks, digging her feet into the sand as far as they will go, her arms closing around herself in embrace – this my land, my home. But the water rushes in. It sucks away the sand around her feet and withdraws, leaving them uprooted, defenceless. She kicks at the sand aimlessly. She looks back.

And then, she sees him. He is coming down from the village. She has dreamt of instant bonding, something flowing from him to her. She walks up and stops directly before him, claiming his attention. He has to know her; he has to acknowledge her – at least.

'Priya?' Her voice is urgent.

It seems he does not hear. Stepping aside and away from her, he resumes walking. Nonplussed, she tries again. She catches hold of his sleeve and tugs. He seems not to notice it, or her. She glimpses his glazed eyes. Then he moves on. He turns towards Simon's house. He enters the gloom, and closes the front door. She watches helplessly, then returns to Simon.

'Let him be, he's not too well this morning, missy,' Simon says. 'Maybe you can come back tomorrow? Where are you staying?'

'Ceyshores,' she mutters. She turns back towards the hotel. Past the stretch of beach studded here and there with cabanas overhung with coconut fronds. She spots a sliver of white skin on a balcony, a leg stretched out. A bare-chested man bends over the rails, so he can observe her better. A train chug-chugging looms around the corner. It is full of men, faceless, white sarongs or black trousers, hanging out of open doors, clinging to windows. She tries to control the beach cloth. The men whistle catcalls. The train crawls. She runs faster, behind the thickness of watekeiya trees.

She sees Paul on the hotel's private beach, and walks towards him. His is a comforting presence. He'd come up to her a few days before, smiling, stepping over his luggage at reception. He'd been garlanded with marigolds. Was she from Australia? A koala munched a gum leaf on her T-shirt. She'd shaken his vigorous hand. He bet there was no way she could say she was Australian and get away with it here, in Sri Lanka? I mean, who'd believe her? She shook her head uncertainly. And laughed. Was he on holiday? She looked around for a wife and three children. Working holiday, he said, writing up a series on tourism in down south Sri Lanka. She thought his eyes lingered on hers, but couldn't be sure.

Now he leans over the hotel's fence, and tips his sunhat to her. She begins to relax – she's on familiar ground. He's been looking out for her, he says. Will she have breakfast with him? And where has she been so early in the morning? But Aruni is still protective of her past. She tells him, yes, she'd like to have breakfast with him but not where she's been. He smiles, blue eyes crinkling at the edges. When she had first gone to school in Australia, she had sat next to a little blonde girl. For a long time after that, she had wished for herself pale-pink skin and sea-blue eyes.

As out of nowhere, a few young men collect around them, just outside the fence. They size up the young girl in her flimsy cloth, and try to catch her eye, to measure her wealth from the wristwatch and backpack. They glance at the man, this white man who looks much older than the girl. They assess the relationship. Aruni returns their looks without shyness.

'Missy, how are you?' they greet her in Sinhalese. She returns the greeting stiffly. They guffaw at her accent.

One of them steps forward, taking control. 'My name is Premasiri. Who is the white gentleman? Is he your husband?'

'No,' she says looking sideways at Paul. 'He's at the hotel. He's from Australia.' They shake hands with Paul across the fence, each one in turn.

She translates the exchange to Paul – how they mistook her for his wife. That'd be right! – he raises his eyebrows. But lets it pass.

The boys speak in English now. 'We can show you turtles, black and white and brown turtles, turtles laying eggs, and beautiful corals at the bottom of the sea. We take missy and sir in glass-bottom boat?'

'All right, some other time, maybe,' Aruni replies, drawn to their friendliness.

The boys sidle up to Paul. 'Cheap, sir, very cheap. Special price for you.'

Paul takes out a cigarette. The boys cluster closer. He offers them the pack. They use his lighter to light up. Premasiri tells Paul he can purchase a new lighter for him, when this one dries up.

'Thanks, mate, I'll get back to you on that,' Paul replies.

'At half price for someone beautiful like you, missy,' Premasiri says, returning the lighter to Aruni. Her fingers curl around its warmth, and she smiles. This time, Paul understands without translations.

The beach gets used to Aruni sitting on the sand by Simon. In the old days, Simon says whimsically, disciples always sat at the feet of the guru. Occasionally Priya is there too, though always a little distance away, perhaps leaning against the coconut tree behind Simon. They seem positioned in an elusively connected triangle.

Once in a way, one or two women might squat nearby to relieve aching arms of plastic bags full of tourist ware. Simon pauses his story in mid-sentence and sells them a kurumba at half price. They glance at Aruni, and nudge one another with an innuendo that only Priya and Simon understand. They regard her with vendor-sharp eyes. Often she buys something she does not need – a batik cloth, a finely crafted miniature of a boat with the sails strung up, an ornament box polished a mottled brown. Aruni knows she is paying more than she should. Simon tells her so. But she pays anyway, without bargaining – perhaps these women had been her mother's friends. When she gives what they ask, their faces soften with weary smiles.

Simon introduces her to them. 'This is someone from Priya's family. Our Mala's daughter,' he says, 'visiting us from Australia.'

But they are mostly interested to know about the rich country. Could she help someone's son apply for a visa in Australia? Was it true that a carpenter there gets more salary in a month than a lawyer gets in a year in this country? Then, a woman remembers vaguely the way Priya's family was wiped out all in one year. But not much more than that. When she walks away, Aruni follows. But the woman is already searching for rich tourists. She shrugs and walks off, her shoulders burdened with bags.

Taking a walk, Paul pauses to photograph the beach – catamarans against the brilliant twilight skies, the delicate footprints of birds on wet sand. He shifts to the poetry behind eyes and lips, the glint of a silver cross on a chain of beads against a woman's sweat-shining neck, a small boy cuffed by an older man for jumping unpropitiously over a length of fishing net. And he photographs Aruni as, listening to Simon, she stretches out on the sand, shielding her eyes from the sun as it sails into the past. Sometimes Paul sits with her, drinking from a kurumba, wanting to understand the language. A kite with a long frilly tail dips and flips, dips and flips, making red waves in the sky.

Simon and Aruni recede from the ebb and flow of life on the beach. They enter a world where all things revolve in slow motion. And Aruni is a child again, being led into this other life. She lies in her father's lap, her head snuggled into his shoulder, and listens to his voice as the fire crackles and spits in the winter's chill in the faraway land.

– Once upon a time, Aruni, down south in Sri Lanka, there was a turtle that loved the beach . . .

The touch of his fingers running through her hair. She turns sideways, on her elbow, so she can see Simon's face as he recollects.

The storm had cleared a little while before, and the wind that had threatened to tear down the house had subsided. Little Nirmala was sitting on the front doorstep, her chin balanced on her knees. She sang softly, the firefly song, as softly as she could, so her father wouldn't wake up and shout at her. But she could hear nice warm sounds coming from the kitchen area where her mother was tending the fire to boil water for tea. And then her attention was caught. It was a baby turtle dropped off the sky with the rain. It had fallen on its back and lay squirming, its limbs seeking to connect with more than air.

She rushed up, and seeing this, her younger brother Priya came out to join her. Like her shadow he was, the way he trailed her. She turned the baby turtle right side up and sat beside it on the sand. Now it lay inert, as still as a stone. Priya wanted to prod it and turn it upside down again. But Mala smacked his hand. After a while, he ran away to trample the waves. Mala squatted by patiently, singing her best song, enticing the turtle to take a few clumsy steps. She went back into the house to get it something to eat. When she returned with a few fish heads the beach boys had got it. She screamed as they threw it like a ball from one to the other over her head. Priya heard her and rushed back to her side. Mala sat back on her haunches and wailed loudly until her mother came out to scold her.

'Child, that miserable creature is better dead,' Asilin said. 'Or else when it grows as big as a house, it will be cut up for raw meat.' In her spare time, Asilin sold turtle meat to rich people. But Mala would not be consoled. She told Priya that she wanted to be a mother turtle, out of contact with everyone on the beach, at the bottom of the sea. And she'd spin a long tale for the four-year old Priya who listened, mouth agape. She giggled then, and wiped her tears, and in a little while they wandered off in search of some other distraction.

'Look at this child, she must always try to do the impossible,' said Asilin, as she selected the smaller fish for her basket in the half-light of dawn. 'Aney Simon, go and bring her back,' she'd say.

And as he walked towards her daughter, Asilin would say to Prancina, who was helping her – wasn't it strange how faithful Simon was to her family. He was not a relative after all, not from her side of the family, or from her children's father's side. If he heard her, Simon turned round to smile. And that made Asilin preen because, just by associating with them, Simon lent her family some respectability.

Prancina offered Asilin a betel leaf with a morsel of areca nut and lime paste. As they chewed, they gossiped desultorily about why Simon was not married. He must be well over thirty-five years old now. Soon he would be past having a woman. If he did not hurry up, he'd die a lonely man in that nice cement house of his. Prancina said that if she had a marriageable daughter she'd cast her net over him. The two women chuckled, spat out red betel juice, and resumed their work.

On chubby legs, Mala ran to the flapping fish. It was a small white mora, just freed by the men, struggling frantically to get its breath of air and leap back into the sea. The general commotion around the net offered her all the freedom in the world.

'Poor fish,' she crooned. 'You come home with me.' She danced around the fish until she caught hold of its tail, then skipped away towards the sea. She splashed into the waves and let it go. Waving her arms in the air, she shouted at it to come back and visit her. But the fish rushed out of her reach. Her laughter faded, her lips trembled with sadness and she gazed after the fish, wanting it to turn round, make friends with her and refuse to return to its old life.

'Foolish child,' Simon said, coming up and swinging her into his arms, 'don't cry, the fish must go where he belongs. Look how the sun peeps out of the sea, Mala.'

And there she was again, straddling her father's shoulders, and together they hit the sea. She tumbled down, and twirled with tadpole flaps. Jamis reached out to her often, squashed her against him, revelled in her chubby body. Their skins glistened oily with sweat and sea.

He would plop her in, laughing to see her swim around him in her funny flapping stroke, and then, suddenly, lift her out of the water and haul her over his shoulders. And with her small strong fingers clutching his hair they waded further and further in, until they left the waves way behind. They saw a school of silver fish disturbed by a diving gull, turtles frolicking in the deeper waters. They watched kissing turtles. That sent Jamis into a great fit of laughter. And it made Mala laugh too, full of glee. She felt so exuberant, sitting up there on top of her world. She wound her arms around his neck and buried her face in his long wet hair. She was a quick passionate little thing, and she loved her father more than anyone else.

Those were the best days, those days when Mala and Priya were small children. Mala had a box full of remnant cloth. With her tongue caught at the edge of her lips, she drew the outlines of a girl-doll, a boy-doll and a baby-doll on a piece of old cardboard. Priya cut them out with the razor blade. 'Make sure you get the heads in a good round shape,' she chuckled, tickling him. 'Last time, the father came out with a square head like yours.' Her eyes shone with the joy of playing house. Priya gazed up at her. His day was suddenly filled with the magic of Mala in a sparkling mood.

Mala cut out dresses for the dolls, and fixed them on. She painted their faces with stubs of crayon. Red and yellow and blue. Lots of red. The dolls were dressed to go visiting. The mother and father dolls on either side with their hands lovingly pressed together on the handle of the pram. The baby in socks and shoes and a dotted bib. How grand they all looked! They stepped out proudly, Priya steering a matchbox car alongside the little procession. Mala had daubed his lips with pink crayon. Sitting on the bench in the yard, their six-year-old twin sisters awaited them with small trays filled with paper cups and saucers, and plates with fat slices of sand-iced cake. They suppressed their laughter at Priya's painted clown-face, and Mala tottering in shoes too big. But the visit ended abruptly. Their mother was yelling at Mala to wash the rice and keep it on the fire, or they could all have sand-cakes for lunch.

Squatting at the back of the house, and swirling the rice in the nambiliya, Mala tried to work out why washing play-rice was so much more fun than washing real rice. Large tears dropped out of her eyes as she threw the water out of the nambiliya and felt for the grit still clinging to its grooves. The water splashed on Simon's sandals as he happened to walk by. He stopped a moment and watched her.

'Are you looking for Priya? He ran to the butik to get something for our mother, aiye,' she said to him unhappily. In those days Simon was not actively looking for Priya.

'I will have the convent car this evening. I'll take you and Priya for a drive – so finish all your work like a good girl, and be ready,' he said gently, and Mala returned to the rice as if Mother Mary had suddenly dropped a handful of pearls in there.

After a good catch, the families got together by the catamarans in the evening. The men drank toddy mixed in arrack, and the women brought over fried sprats, and prawn vadai. Some of the women drank openly with the men. The beach spread around and beyond, in silver-edged shadow. The surf broke easily and spread wide luminous waves. The air was so clear there seemed to be nothing between sky and beach. The moon, Mala said, showing it to Simon, have I ever seen a moon so big, Simon aiye? Like a lover's smile, Simon thought to himself.

Moonbeams showered white flowers. Priya reached out his hands to catch them.

The men began to sing as the toddy hit them, and it was on one of those nights that the boy Rathu caught Mala's hand and took her behind a boat. She could not have been more than twelve years old at the time. Simon saw Rathu draw her to him. He saw Mala savouring the sour sweetness of his toddy-filled breath. Simon wanted to call her to him, but he went on sitting at a distance, watching the two figures. With no warning at all, the wind began to rise, blowing salt and sand into eyes, black clouds rushed across the sky, and the rain pelted down. The men ran drunkenly for shelter leaving the women to pick up the empty dishes and glasses.

Simon waited for Mala. She was soaked through when she came out from behind the boat. Squeezing the water from her skirt, and with a backward glance, she ran towards the house. As she paused at the threshold, he could see her body, nakedly illuminated by the light within.

They'd tell stories sitting on the beach, Simon, Mala and Priya. The wind played with her hair, and flicked a bit of sparkle off a lonely star. She hid it in her palm and turned to Simon, and he caught its light in the corners of her eyes. Did she laugh then, or brush her face lightly against his shoulder, move just that moment closer? They'd listen to her song.

Listen, that's your mother's song, Simon says. Aruni holds her breath, but it is the wind rasping in the scrub behind them. She sinks within herself. Her mother belongs, has always belonged, to others. Would she never whisper to her as she did to these people who released their memory of her as if she belonged to them, exclusively?

But she asks Simon to continue, as she lies on the sand, and draws up her knees. Simon bends to pull the parted bath cloth around her. 'You must be a bit careful on this beach, missy,' he says lightly.

He smiles at her lack of self-consciousness. But the smile dies; he remembers the way her mother had been, so absorbed in her own knowing.

'How can you understand any of this, missy?' Simon asks Aruni one day. 'How can you know her like we did? What made you come back after all this time?'

Unwillingly, Aruni begins a fragment of her own life, lived away from home, in the adopted world. 'Once I heard a song in Melbourne. My father had told me, a few days before, that my real mother had been a fisher-girl from the south of Sri Lanka.

When I heard that song, I knew I had to come here and find out more about her.'

'Let's see, sing it for us then,' Simon says.

A fisherman is adrift on the high seas. He rests back in his boat and succumbs to solitude. And then, from the faraway land, a beckoning lamp sets aglow a woman's tenderness. Come, she sings, we were lost but are found in the seven seas.

Simon hums the tune. They all sang it in those days, or whistled it, ending their nights with it. And he remembers its echo in Priya's voice, the tremor with which Priya trailed the last words, and in Priya's father's voice, too. But they sang it differently. They knew about being cast adrift. They'd succumbed to its isolation, dreamed of a woman's arms raised to light a lamp in the darkened world. Aruni's voice skims over meaning. It reminds Simon of the rough bubble sounds that the fish made when they surfaced far out in the sea. He clears his throat. The song ends abruptly. Aruni's eyes, with their usual look of welled-up tears, are cast out to sea.

Priya comes up, and leans against the tree behind them, cleaning his teeth with an ekel. He barely looks at Aruni. But she wonders whether he has come out of Simon's verandah because he recognised the song. She turns to him, but he doesn't say a word. There is a silence about him that is almost tangible. The sea is everywhere, spreading and spreading and roaring and heaving, flooding their lives.

Sometimes Aruni does not see Priya for days. That's when his house claims him. It lies not too far away down the beach from Simon, and is almost in ruins. The thatched roof flutters in the slightest breeze, and people say that the next monsoon will bring it down forever. The side lime wall is intact though. Priya mends the roof now and then, pushing a new coconut frond in between the sticks where the old one has worn away. He opens the wooden windows, and the sunlight shafts in. But the walls are disintegrating with neglect. Priya wanders from room to kitchen, searching for what's alive. All the love, after all, is also in this house, crouching and whimpering in corners. Sometimes he takes a white man into the house. Then the younger boys squat outside, gossiping and peeping between the slats in the walls until the man emerges, and then they trail him, trying to sell him some ganja or hashish.

The evening casts long shadows across the beach. Simon turns to Aruni and she hears him as in a dream.

'There, look over there, missy. Look at the lihiniya birds rushing to their nests in the rock island! If you were closer, you'd shut your ears for the noise they made.'

His voice is low, and she has to strain to catch the words.

'Sometimes,' he says, 'I can hear her breath around me, I can even touch it as the wind breaks it up into sobs.'

Paul enters the dining hall dressed in a sarong. Aruni walks round him with a proprietary air, tucking in a bit here, loosening a bit there. She orders breakfast for them, introduces him to kola kanda. He looks at it bemused. He has been content with bacon and eggs. It's leaf-rice porridge, Paul, and an aphrodisiac, she teases. Paul sips it, thinking that he could acquire a taste for it. She offers him a bite of juggery to sweeten it. She tells him that she's acquiring a new hobby, collecting interesting sea debris.

She never has much to show when she returns to the hotel. She does not like it when he joins her. At times she walks at sunrise, then at sunset. He watches from the ledge at the far end of the hotel garden. She squats on the sand, regards things. He takes photographs. She leaps beyond the hotel's private beach. Her long brown legs glisten with sand, and her midriff shows wider between bikini top and shorts. Premasiri and his friends join her most times, and Paul sees that Aruni welcomes them. Often she and Premasiri walk ahead, and the gang lags behind. Everyone knows the beach is not safe for tourists, local or foreign. But Paul is reluctant to invade her space, and watches from afar. He is generally around when she returns.

'There was a dead jellyfish on the beach, Paul, and I saw little fish in its tummy. I tried to get them out but they spattered on the sand, all dead. Poor little fish.' She sits down by his side at lunch.

'And what's the big deal about a beached jellyfish, Aruni? They live in the sea and die on the beach. It's that small matter of life and death, remember?'

But he is silenced by her expression of twisted hurt. 'Oh I don't know. I get so miserable, Paul, sometimes I don't even know what I'm crying about. Or what I'm searching for here. Do you?' She presses her face into her hands.

He watches helplessly.

'Here, drink this,' he says, touching a glass to

her lips. She circles her cold fingers over his and drinks. She quivers out of her mood, as if shedding a skin.

Letting her alone, Paul walks to the ledge. The mid-afternoon sun bleaches the sea. Paul looks back at Aruni, a bit concerned. But she already has her earphones on. Gradually, she stretches out and closes her eyes. Her head begins to swing in a heightened staccato to the rhythms and beats, the pauses and the tempos. It takes him back to Sue. When he left her, she had been stuck on Coolplay. Coldplay, Dad, she'd say patiently, eyes rolling skyward. He wonders whether they lived less fully – he and Sue, and Jo. Was his life bland because it held no mysteries? Twenty years of marriage. Forty-five years old. No midlife crisis in sight. He smiles, happy with his life. This heat wave, he sighs, flapping his open shirt for a breath of non-existent air, this heat today, can it go away?

Paul gives Aruni a pretty flower he has plucked off a crack in the ledge. She spreads its delicate petals and shows him the deeper blue of its heart. She holds it alongside his eyes. The exact same colour, she says.

She brushes it on her lips, consciously provocative. Lazily Paul reciprocates. Nearby, a woman is sweeping dried leaves into a heap. Paul asks her for a clip to fix the flower in Aruni's hair. And did this flower have a name?

'We call it mini-mal, sir, – funeral flower,' the woman translates for Paul. 'If I were you, missy, I would not pin that flower in my hair,' she tells Aruni in Sinhalese. 'It grows in cemeteries and lonely places.'

Paul takes a step closer to fix the flower.

Aruni suffers the flower in her hair. But as soon as she is alone, she removes it. It is bruised and already fading in the heat. She breaks it up into bits to ward off evil spirits. The breeze disperses them here and there – spots of blue on the grass. She sits inert, watching them, and her skin crawls with unpropitious imaginings.

Aruni offers Paul fragments of her life. How had she heard that she had been adopted? Oh, she says, it was surreal. She'd always sensed festering secrets. But the earliest memory, Aruni? Do you want to remember?

Well, a day in the park with her mother. An OK day, nothing out of the ordinary. Swings and seesaws. Preoccupied mother, querulous child.

A lady nicely dressed, came up and spoke to the mother.

'Neela, I have not seen you for so long. How long? Eight years? I heard about the new child and all. Is this the one? What's her name?'

'Aruni.'

The flippant voice of the stranger, the prying eyes. Aruni tried to hide behind her mother. But the lady insisted on holding up her chin, raising her face for inspection. Aruni offered her dark unfriendly smile. A frown line of disappointment etched on the lady's forehead.

'Oh, she's so different from your own . . . your other daughter. What was her name again?'

'Kumari,' her mother said. She gripped Aruni's fingers so tight, Aruni wanted to cry out in pain.

'Oh yes, Kumari, I'd forgotten. I was so sad about her death. Meant to write, but we were in London at the time. It was from my sister that I heard about this one.'

Neela's fingers fell away. Aruni stuck her hands behind her back. She wanted to poke out her tongue at the stranger. But when she looked up, the veiled secret stared with monster eyes right down at her. She ran away out of reach of the lady.

That night, Aruni listened to her mother tell her father, 'I'm sick of this country where everyone knows everyone, and everyone must know everything. Let's sign those migration papers and go away to Australia. Might be better there, where no one knows anything.'

Her father looked her way, but she'd turned to the Lego, building her red and yellow house, looking for windows and doors, and the garden of flowers. For the first time, she excluded the father and mother toys from the garden, and left at the gate a child about to run out . . .

That was when she had begun to understand. In her dreams she just walked around and around. She found herself in an open field. She lay down. The sky was blue, blue without end. Blue is the colour of sadness. She saw blue flowers turn white in the sky. White is the colour of death. She hears her father sing of the dead daughter, Kumari, being carried to the cemetery shrouded in white. She watches Neela weep and pull out the flowers that blossomed on the grave.

Aruni curled up into herself. She wept as if someone close to her had died. Something inside me died, she says now to Paul, someone I had known all my life. I don't know who was reborn in the husk of my body, Aruni says. But I knew I belonged somewhere else.

Paul is as surprised as she is when he holds out his hand to her. And she lays hers in his trustingly. Sitting together, they count the dilapidated boats lying sideways, abandoned to their sandy graves, and imagine how they once had braved the seas on nights like tonight.

In Melbourne, a recent memory. The shine of lights. Waves lolling against St Kilda pier. And boats resting on their waterbeds, making music, haunting pipe music as the wind flowed through. Aruni's father leans across the small table. He reveals to her, at last, the secret of her birth, gives her a note and a photograph. And unfolds the adoption papers. She stares down at these claims on her. She draws away from her father's protection, and is aware of the lonely freedom of a seedling pushing out of the earth to claim its new life.

'Listen to the music,' Aruni says in a faraway voice. 'If you listen carefully, you'll hear the music the boats make. Like someone playing a flute.' A host of small stars are fallen in the sea.

A waiter comes up to chat, and tells Aruni that on the clearest days, you can spot Adam's Peak on the landside.

'I've seen the sun rise from the top of Adam's Peak, Paul,' Aruni says later. 'It's incredible, the way this molten ball of fire worships the peak before it rises. We climbed it on one visit to Sri Lanka. We climbed a zillion steps right through the night, and reached the peak just before dawn, and man, was it something to see! My legs hurt like they were going to drop. Everyone was awestruck and fell down on their knees. They say that's where Lord Buddha first set foot in the country, and that's why the sun worships it before rising.'

'I thought you were extreme unction Catholics,' Paul teases.

'Neela is a Buddhist. My father is a Catholic. My real mother, Mala, was also a Catholic. I have no idea what I am. Everyone's a bit of everything when they're Sri Lankan.'

It was the evening of the Christmas concert. Mala was dressed earlier than was required. She draped the blue robes around her, and over her shoulders. Priya fell back in admiration. He'd never seen anyone so splendid, so tall and graceful. Turning this way and that, she regarded as much as she could of herself. Climbing up on a chair, Priya removed the mirror off its hook, and held it so she could see her face without strain. The bright blue satin was soft to the touch, and heightened the flush on her face. She drew the white shawl over her hair, and folded her palms. She smiled gloriously into the small spotted mirror. She was to play Mother Mary. The sisters said she was a good girl, doing all that work for them in the chapel. Yes, they said, their chapel maid Mala deserved to be Mary over all the regular students.

When she was ready to leave, Simon gave her a lift in the convent car, so she would not have to walk with her trailing robes. 'Can I sit in the back seat like a lady?' she asked, attired in her borrowed finery. 'Yes, madam,' Simon said. He even opened the door for her, so she could glide in without wrinkling her costume. Priya jumped in the front seat. He kept turning round to gaze at Mala's beauty. He puffed with pride. For that whole evening he was going to bask in the glory of being Our Lady's little brother.

And how sacred she looked with all the stage lights falling on her. She knelt, her eyes devoutly and maternally cast down on the infant doll in the crib. A special light trembled in the air close to her, lighting up her face with a golden glow. And there was Joseph standing by her protectively, leaning on his crook. It seemed to Priya, as he crawled around the crib with his lamb-ears, singing 'Jesu Bilinda' with gusto, that Joseph was not playing his part at all well. He kept staring at Mary. Even the audience noticed it and treated Joseph to a few wolf-whistles and catcalls.

As the stage dimmed, and the lights came up in the hall, Mala picked up the baby Jesus, and curled it in the crook of her arm. Joseph drew protectively close. There was loud applause, and Mala looked up at last, seeking her family scattered about the hall. She saw her father standing at the edge of the crowd, close to the stage. His eyes were shining, wet, and full of prayer. His palms were clasped in simple humility. She smiled with wonderment because everyone knew he never went anywhere near the church if he could help it, not even on Christmas night. She glimmered for him.

The concert ended with a fancy dress parade. There was a doctor with a stethoscope, a nurse in her ticking-cloth uniform and canvas shoes. There were two or three fishermen with pingos that they swayed proudly as they walked. There were kings, and angels with lopsided paper wings.

And then, Mala. This time she was dressed in the old cloth that her mother wore for selling turtle meat. It was stained with dried blood. Mala's face looked parched, her lips hanging loose. Smudged lipstick from Mother Mary's make-up still stuck to her cheeks. She held a stick to aid her walk. Tiredly, she dragged from the left to the right of the stage and then stopped in the centre. She sang a beggar's song in an unfamiliar older woman's voice. It was as if she knew the meaning of the song of that beggar woman going mad with the sorrows that life heaped on her. Standing in the wings, Priya saw the women around him wipe their eyes. In the end, Mala came forward and bowed. But as she limped off, she stuck out her tongue roguishly at him. He laughed and laughed then, clapping madly.

'Missy, do you know the meaning of your mother's name?' Simon asks.

'Nirmala? Never thought about it. I know the meaning of mine – names with meaning are ridiculous. Parents just land all their expectations on children, naming them after some silly dream they have.'

But Simon sinks into a reverie. 'Mala,' he says, 'Mala means garland.'

'Her name was Nirmala, it means pure, pure like the Mother of Jesus,' Priya says from behind.

They turn towards him in surprise. He speaks so seldom that they often forget his presence. His eyes are unfocused. He turns stiffly and limps down the beach. He picks up a coconut that the sea has thrown out, and lets it drop back on the sand. The waves sucked the coconuts into the sea, devoured their insides and then tossed out the husks. Sucked in, thrown out. Sucked in, thrown out.

'Lost lonely things,' Aruni says to Simon.

'But why?' Simon asks. 'Why must you always belong to someone or to someplace? Why can't you find a home right inside yourself? A restfulness so private that no thief may enter it, where you can withdraw when you want to? It is enough for me, if I have that. I am free, to roam the seas if I want to. For this I give blessings.'

But Aruni must retrieve the coconut, and throw it far inland where it may grow a seedling, shielded by the scrub. She also wants to claim Priya's attention. She stands, wiping the sand off her legs, to go to him.

'Let him be, missy,' Simon warns her.

'But he knows all that happened, so why doesn't he tell me anything, Simon?'

'Let him be, missy.' Simon repeats. 'He doesn't want to remember, can't you see that? No one wants to remember, and you keep asking your questions.'

'Why can't you call me Aruni?' She turns to him petulantly, her eyes still on Priya. 'Why do you say missy missy all the time and treat me like a stranger?

I am not a stranger. I belong here, I belong to him, to
Priya. He is my uncle.'

'I am just an ordinary man who used to drive
the convent car. Priya is a nomad on the beach. You
are a lady, missy. In two months you will be gone, safe
where you belong. You will forget all about us. We
are from different worlds. Why don't you leave us
alone?'

'But the worlds have to meet and cross. Don't
you see that? They have to meet and cross.'

'Why? Because missy says so?'

Aruni digs a stick into the sand. She watches a
hermit crab scrambling sideways in a borrowed shell.
She throws sand at it. Disturbed, it sheds the shell and
escapes into a small hole.

Simon observes her erratic response to the
beach. He remembers how Mala would let small
creatures crawl up her legs, almost up to her thighs.
The way her skin danced as they tightened their small
claws on her. How she'd gently pick them off, and let
them wander away. He leans back in his chair and
closes his eyes. He wants to slip back in time, to the
days before Aruni materialised at his feet. He feels
thrust into memories that he had loved and buried.

But then another image rises. He is visiting the

graveyard. He's brought flowers, the small sweet jasmines that Mala strung into garlands for the church statues, and has placed them carefully by the wooden cross that bears her name. He wipes the dust from it with his palm. He weeds the mound of earth, and carefully sweeps on it the coconut-frond design. He sits down by the grave. He remembers the way she'd been, and how she'd disappeared from their lives. And how they'd finally given up their search for her by burying her memory in this unknown grave.

As he gets ready to leave, Mala smiles, and rubs against his chest, takes his hand in both hers, and blesses him for the flowers. But he knows that time has passed, and these are not her hands. He looks down and finds Aruni's fingers curling around his. She gazes at him with her mother's eyes. When the contact begins to ache, Simon removes his hand. Hurt as her mother had been by his rejection, Aruni walks away.

In the night, she has a nightmare. She's seen the spattered jellyfish on the shingled beach. A lonely fear grips her. The airconditioner is dead and the room is stifling hot. But she shivers with chill, drawing the sheet up to her neck. She drifts back into a half sleep and jolts awake dripping with sweat. She has to get out of the room. She opens the door and stands on the balcony, breathing in and out, in and out. A few birds rush out of the almond tree, circle around looking for daybreak, and, cheated, squawk back to their perches. The air is warm and salty. She looks down the corridor and sees light still seeping out from under Paul's door.

She walks to it and knocks. Paul glances at his watch – it is very late – but he invites her in, reluctantly. He offers her a glass of brandy. She sits on his bed and swirls it against the light. It glows with amber depths . . . Her father had clasped an amber pendant around her neck on her eighteenth birthday. Neela stood as always in the doorway, looking on from an unbridgeable distance. Aruni had wrapped her arms around her father, before going over to Neela. Neela touched the pendant, and held out her cheek to be kissed. In her eyes Aruni saw what she had always seen, but had never defined. Now she knew what it was – the truth of her birth. They stood close together with nothing to say. Then as of habit, Neela glanced beyond her at her father, and they shared their life before her birth: the dregs of un-resolved hurt, the guilt-riddled withdrawal. A few months later, just before she left for Sri Lanka, Aruni had ground the pendant into the earth. She lies back in Paul's bed and closes her eyes.

Paul removes the glass from her hand. She turns on her side, away from him, and sleeps at last. He sits by her for a long time after she is silent. It may have been wiser, he thinks, drawing the covering sheet over her, to have left her well alone. For her, and for him. He has a life, he thinks, a solid life to return to. He returns to his papers splayed on the table. He closes his laptop, switches out the lamp, and lies down on the divan. His work is almost complete, and he will have a couple of months at least in which to do nothing. He thinks of other assignments – he'd send for Jo and Sue when a holiday became possible like this – Edinburgh and Dublin. Jo packed up to her ears in wool, blowing white mist in the frozen air. The cold of bed sheets, the heat of fireside sex.

Paul lies awake, missing his wife, missing her breath, her way of climbing into bed. He misses his body curving towards hers with that wonderful intimacy of habit. But he knows that he will not invite her to Sri Lanka. He avoids questioning it. He listens instead to the night stalking the beach. He hears an occasional shout and long-drawn whistles. Restless, he walks to the window and makes out the beach boys sitting astride the ledge. A security guard chats with them. Lit cigarettes glimmer like fireflies. They see him against the light behind, and wave to him. He hears Aruni's name stretched like syrup in their language. Irritated, he draws the curtains.

A few hours later, Paul wakes Aruni with a cup of tea. She blinks in the bright sunshine and pulls herself up into a half-sitting position. Then she hides her face behind her palms, embarrassed.

'Did you know that you sleep with your eyes half open?' Paul asks, leaning forward to draw up the thin strap of her pyjama top from her arm to her shoulder. 'I slept on the divan,' he says. She puts her hand on his.

'Thank you, Paul, you're a mate,' she murmurs.

'S'okay, missy, you owe me one. Let's go down to breakfast,' Paul replies – giving her space.

These days, in the monsoon season, when the boats can't go to sea, one day on the beach is no different from another, Simon explains. But long years ago, missy, before terrorism started up in the country, most of the younger fishermen packed up and went up East during the monsoons. They were nicely established and even had fishing colonies there. They were absent for months, but it was lucrative, and they sent down extra money. That's how Priya's house has one lime plaster wall to it, and that's how the family got their line of electricity.

But then the Tigers started attacking the Sinhalese fisher colonies in the East. Village after village was destroyed. Then Mala's father stopped migrating that way. As the war went on and on, the rich tourists stopped coming over, so all those others in the fishing village who lived off the tourists went empty handed. See, even these days, missy, how the hotels are almost empty, with only the poorer tourists coming in on cheap deals.

When it got really bad, with no money even for a shundu of rice, Jamis would ride his old bicycle a few villages away, and try to join the stilt fishing. But most of the time, the regulars chased him away fearing that a stranger would bring them bad luck. Sometimes they even pushed him off when he tried to climb an unused stilt and, cursing, he would fall back into the water. Then, he got into violent fights and came home bleeding. Once, he was knifed in the shoulder. Then Mala's mother would scold shrilly and tell anyone who'd listen that she'd starve rather than sell any sprat that came from the stilts.

Jamis lay inactive for days after such a brawl, and then his temper flared at the smallest thing. He drank more than usual, with a friend or two who'd drop by with a pot of toddy. He got Asilin to temper some fish and made Mala pass it round, drawing the attention of the other men to her plump body in the ill-fitting dress with its gaping side seams held together by safety pins.

'She's going to be an eyeful, isn't she – and a mouthful, like the tempered fish,' he laughed, his cheeks bulging with the hotly peppered stuff, and tried to pull her onto his lap. Half playfully, not wanting to rouse his anger, Mala pushed him away. Her mother came out then, and cursed the men out of the house. As Asilin walked back in, Jamis would stretch out and pull her by the hand, and she'd reel towards him – laughing a bit but still scolding. He'd begin to undo the pins on her blouse.

Asilin was still a young woman in those days. But she was lean with childbearing and overwork. She sat by the hut in the mornings to rest sometimes, forever holding an infant to her breast. Mala was weaned away only after the twins were born, and then came Priya.

Priya wasn't much to look at, Simon says, a weedy child, sniffling and sniffling. Even when he sucked at his mother's breast, he sniffled. She hardly felt his hunger, and often her breast hung free of his lips. Only his eyes, black and large, were alive, wandering from his mother's face to the coconut fronds waving green feathers against the blue sky. Asilin smiled her tired smile as Mala yelled to her from the sea. They wearied her with their exuberant energy, the man and the little girl.

And then the monsoons ended, and life revolved around the sea all over again. It was a busy expectant time for the men as they readied the boats. They tested their nets, and repaired them with their hooked metal needles. The women did not share their eagerness. They complained when the men hung around idle in the monsoons. But complained again when they had to be released to the sea. Young wives, many of them pregnant, stood around thinking of the lonely nights ahead.

The mudalali was often around, inspecting his boats and nets, reminding his fishermen what they owed him, looking for new recruits among the able-bodied boys just maturing to manhood. He was finding it harder to lease his boats, because the fishermen were getting poorer. So he got more and more stringent. He exhorted heavy interest from them when he loaned them money to lease his boats, and bought the fish they drew in at the lowest price possible. Men like Jamis were bound to him for life in a cycle of poverty.

'Come down to the beach at dawn tomorrow, missy, and you can watch a catch of fish with us.'

'Oh can I, Simon? Can I?' Delighted, she holds on to his arm like a little girl. 'Can I bring Paul?'

'That's good,' Simon says. 'The beach is not always safe – I keep telling you that. Bring Paul sir.' Nice man, Simon thinks, this Paul with his hot mix of colours. Blue eyes and burned red skin, and yellow T-shirt with red elephants. Whenever he came down to the beach with Aruni, Simon offered Paul a kurumba to cool down his skin.

'Not safe, Simon?' Aruni retorts as always. 'Of course it is safe, safe for me. No one will harm me here. I'm among friends. Everyone knows me now.'

They gather at the edge of the sea in small groups, awaiting the catamarans. The women light up their kerosene lamps and dried coconut leaves, guiding the men back home. There is a lot of laughter and joking. Aruni hums her song about the lonely fisherman and the unknown woman. A child toddles up. She bends down, and lifts him in her arms, and is happy when his sister also wants to be carried. She sits with them, and tells her story about the turtle. But the little girl wants something she's not heard before, so Aruni tries a nursery rhyme. The child falls asleep, snug in her lap. The children's mother comes up and tells Aruni about all the hardships. Aruni offers her some money. The woman tucks it away in her blouse and removes the child from her lap.

The beach boys cluster around. Premasiri has brought a present for Aruni – a beautiful coral ornament shaped like a woman. Their fingers touch as they trace its curves and hollows. It glistens like her eyes as she leans forward to kiss his cheek. She thinks of how it might have been for her, had she lived amongst her mother's people. Paul draws near. He wonders whether Aruni knows what she is doing – behaving with such familiarity with these boys who seemed so feral to him. They crack crude jokes, looking suggestively at him.

The boats come in to a flurry of activity. The men on the beach help the fishermen haul in the length of net. They sing their long, drawn-out song, and pull the net to its rhythm. And then they push back the last catamarans from the sea. Paul photographs the men straightening their arched bodies with each wave, up and back, up and back, their hips pressed against the horizontal slats. He moves up for a closer look.

The past could always be retrieved differently. Simon says that the woman sitting on the upturned boat could be Asilin. She was sleepy but welcoming and was content to be sitting there. She watched and sometimes helped sort the fish, after the men hauled in the net. Asilin had often sat on a boat like this, and remembered the way her children clung to her knees or thighs, dependent on her. She remembered suckling Mala, and how greedy for her milk Mala had been. When the twins were born, Mala was nearly two years old, and still wanting to suck my milk, Asilin would say. I had to push her away.

Asilin remembered how Mala loved the changing shades of sunrise – red-gold flowers in the sky. She remembered also, as in an unending nightmare, the bloodied cloth in which Mala had left them her infant.

The way it wrapped round the tiny body, the way it had left patches of faded red on the translucent baby skin. And she remembered her husband's knife, raised against her and the infant. The blood that had oozed from it, fish blood, her blood, his, all mixed in confusion – the reds of hearts breaking. All this she wanted to forget.

But, this was the family, Simon whispers in Aruni's ear, and they managed somehow, like the other beach families. They lived in a meagre hut that looked like all the other huts that housed families like theirs. If you stand at the front door of any one of these shanties, missy, you can see right through – front room, kitchen, out the back door, and across the small patch of yard – into the hut behind.

And that's often what Priya and Mala did when they were old enough. They'd look for their mother and, finding her missing, they'd run away to peep into other houses. Most of the time, when Asilin had to go out selling fish, or help cut turtle meat, she asked a neighbour woman to look after the twins. But she left Priya in Mala's care. Sometimes a kindly woman would serve Mala and Priya half a plate of rice and jadi fish that left them still hungry. Mala would have gladly left Priya behind except that he clung to her with such determination, and set up such a bawl, that it was easier to drag him along.

'You're a nuisance – why don't you go trailing behind our mother?' she'd scold him, but all he would do was sniffle, trying to hang on to her hand and keep up with her swift pace.

'You have got that from your mother, missy – she had the same flowing stride. She moved like a song in the wind.'

Aruni gazes ahead, and works out in her heart the shapes of the people she's getting to know. She sees the crimson-dressed Mala, and the shrinking ragged-edged Priya trailing her. She sees him running to catch up with her, and how she occasionally turns to cuff him with a touch of tenderness, and call him her patiya.

'And bit by bit,' Simon says, 'the family hauled in their sorrow.'

It all began when Mala started to grow up. It was Priya who first noticed the change. Priya who trailed her more and more obsessively. He saw it one morning at the road tap, where they went to wash, after the women had come and gone with their buckets of water for the morning chores. His mother had been shouting at her children to bathe. As usual, she left the burden of Priya to Mala.

There they were then, at the tap, and Mala first bathed Priya with a bowl dipped in the bucket of water. Priya watched the water flow, clean and transparent, cold and fresh, and looked up at his sister as she bent over him. And suddenly he found himself looking at her body under the dress that scooped low at the neck. It was a cast-off that had been passed down to her by the good sisters of the convent, and she loved it because it was light and loose on her skin, and very beautifully scarlet. But it was two sizes too large for her. He could see her breasts, raised, as he had never seen them before. He looked down quickly but would remember them often, like two baby coconuts, he thought, that sometimes dropped off the tree before they ripened, when the night wind got them. Little hard fruit that he and Mala spun round and round on an ekel so they made a funny tukka-tukka sound.

Waiting, forever waiting for his sister to come home, Priya would see her suddenly. And then he'd run to her. He'd walk just behind her, trailing for scraps of affection. He'd run errands for her. He'd squat outside Rathu's house for hours watching for prying eyes when Rathu persuaded Mala inside and got her to draw on his Three Rose cigarettes. If Priya saw anyone approach, he'd hit the wall with his stick, and they'd be quiet for a while, until he gave the all-clear signal.

One day, he saw them through the gaps in the torn curtain. He clung to the window poles and, in the semi darkness, he saw their lips pressed together, moving to some slow, throbbing rhythm. It reminded him of the full-throated song that his sister sang sitting on the bench behind their house. The kiss and the song – Priya's heart felt ready to burst with love.

Mala and Priya waded into the lagoon. In the evenings, they came with Simon to catch lagoon fish for the family's night meal. Mala knotted her skirt high above her knees. The ends still dripped with mud, but she did not care. Simon climbed on the foot-bridge that lay across the lagoon and, from way up there, swirled the dulu net around over his head and threw it. Mala thought he looked like a Hindi film star with the evening sun lighting him up. The net opened out as it fell in the most perfect circle, and shimmered into the water. They moved about in the ripples till the fish settled in. Mala splashed Simon's bare chest. Occasionally she leaned forward and wiped his face with wet palms. And she sang her lagoon song. Simon said that her song lured dozens of fish into his net. Laughing, they would close in, standing thigh-deep in water. Priya swam round and round, dragging in the net's periphery, trapping the fish in its centre. Then Simon drew in the net, twisting it into a rope in his hands. Dozens of small shiny fish would gasp to their death. Always, Mala released a fish or two. This made Simon frown, but he always let her have her way.

The past is alive. Simon sits on the bank. The setting sun spills its magic into the reflections in the water, a man and a girl sway towards each other. The ripples sparkle in widening circles. Suddenly taking a stone, Simon flings it in. The water smashes into shards. The reflections shiver, distort and drown. He hears her lagoon song. I am your water flower. I float in the shine of the moon. Lie in the scent of night, my love, and smell the blossom's heart. A garland of flowers I'll weave, my love . . .

On a Sunday, Mala awakened before dawn. She took her bath cloth off the string overhead and her soap box. It was still dark when she opened the back door, slowly, quietly, so as not to awaken anyone, particularly not Priya. She did not want him dragging along behind her, pulling on her dress and hindering all her movements. At this time there was no one about. Even the mangy stray dogs were asleep. They scratched now and then, stirring up small clouds of dust. She picked up a fresh baby coconut, dropped off the tree in the night, and tied it to the end of her dress. At the road tap, Mala wrapped the bath cloth around herself and slid out of her skirt and blouse.

Dawn unfurled in red petals of light. Mala's lips parted. She swayed her body this way and that as though she were standing before a long mirror. She unfolded her hair from its plait and drew her fingers through the long wavy strands. She placed her hands on her hips, and stretched towards unseen arms. She pouted and cast down her eyes. She mourned and a flush crept up her cheeks. She hummed a tune she'd heard on the wireless, recalling lustrous eyes hypnotising a young boy in his dream. Half smiling, she opened the bath cloth slightly, letting the breeze fondle her skin, and watched her breasts harden and rise. She heard a sound then, perhaps a footstep, and she wrapped the cloth around herself slowly, inviting the eyes hidden in the shadows to taste her skin. She imagined them narrowing and glowing in the dark, as she'd seen her father's eyes when he regarded her in a drunken mood. An instant before he turned away, he would look at her as if he knew who she was, and she understood that her body was made for more than the shapeless dresses that the convent shielded it with. Secretly she hungered for this knowledge. She looked around furtively, and disappointed to find herself alone, opened the tap and waited until the water filled the bucket. As she bathed, she let in the imagined eyes beneath the soaked cloth. She pressed the water out of the cloth by placing her palms against her breasts and drawing them down, down to her knees until the cloth moulded the body. Until, in that faint light, devouring eyes could savour her nakedness.

Languidly, Mala bathed, lifting buckets of water easily over her head. She soaped herself, sliding her hand over her body, holding the cloth up against her breasts with her other hand. The soap slithered to the slab of cement on which she stood, and she pushed it away with her foot, into the dirt. Someone on the beach had given her a sachet of shampoo and she lathered her hair with it, relishing its fragrance. She wished she never had to use the horrible carbolic soap. She could see what it had done to her mother's hair that now cringed, scanty and dull against her neck.

She changed back into her clothes. She squeezed the water out of the bath cloth and swish-swished it in the air.

She crept back into the house. She reached up to the small mirror and combed down her hair, wiping the comb afterwards on her skirt to dry it. Releasing the few strands of hair come loose on it, she wound them round her finger and then pushed the curl into the cloth bag hanging by the mirror. She brought her face up against the mirror, and smiled for it, sultry and heavy lidded. She longed to be in some other, scented place.

She looked round the room. Priya lay close to their mother, as if he wanted to creep back into her womb. The two younger sisters were entangled in each other's arms. Mala watched them sleeping, all these people to whom she belonged and who belonged to her. She knelt by Priya and left the little coconut at his side. He muttered in his sleep and she moved quickly away. She had things to do. But her mother's face, careworn even in sleep, was chiselled into her heart as she slipped out of the door.

Mala entered the convent gates in a subdued mood. She carried her missal and her rosary and faded white veil. She wore a loose shift that fell below her knees. To accentuate the shape of her body, she had tied a string around her waist. She was on her way to get the chapel ready for morning mass. On the way she stopped at the refectory. Sister Anne's unsmiling face could do with a sprinkling of sugar, Mala thought, taking the proffered bun with a humble smile. She bit into the sugary crust and was satisfyingly aware that, within the precinct of the convent, she was free of her brother; she could eat her bun all by herself without his sniffle stirring her conscience. She saw Father Lucien walking towards her with his head thoughtfully down, his hands clasped behind his scapular. He suddenly raised his eyes. The new candles had arrived and were ready in the box in the sacristy, he said. He stopped to inquire after her family.

'Tell your mother that the Federation students have brought in some clothes that might fit you all,' he said.

'Yes, Father,' Mala said with eyes cast down.

Fleetingly she regretted having missed them, those smart girls from the rich Colombo schools. She liked looking at them as they clustered in the chapel to organise the used clothes they had brought with them for distribution among the poor fisher children. Mala would stare enviously at their impeccable white uniforms, their shoes and socks. Standing half-hidden in the sacristy, she imagined she was one of those girls, talking in English so fluently with Father.

'Has Priya dropped out of school as well, child? First you, and now your brother. What do your mother and father say about it?' Father Lucifer asked.

'I don't know, Father,' Mala said indifferently, twisting the end of the string dangling from her waist. School, and who could afford school? But she said nothing. She knew that Father understood.

And then, suddenly remembering, 'Aney Father,' she pleaded, 'will you bless my new rosary? I got it at the Sunday fair.'

Father Lucien blessed the rosary warmly, including her in the blessing, and gave it back to her.

'Say a decade for me.' He smiled, and went his way.

Mala gazed at the rosary lying in her palm. Its glass beads enchanted her. She'd selected this one specially from all the others hanging in the stall because each decade was set in ruby-red beads, and the cross was studded as well. How it caught the rays of the sun now, and glowed like drops of blood in the hollow of her palm. She looked back at Father Lucien. He was the nicest of all the priests and nuns she knew. She would say a special prayer for him, for the clothes he gave them, for the love he showered on them expecting nothing in return. For a moment, her thoughts dwelt on the mudalali from whom her father leased his catamaran. Her mother kept them all out of his way. He was a shark, Asilin said often enough, and lived not only off his fishermen but off their wives and daughters as well, when he got the chance.

Mala draped her veil, tied it in a knot below her chin, and entered the cool dark sanctuary. She dipped her fingers in the little angel-faced bowl of holy water and genuflected. The chapel was all hers in these early morning hours and she relished her aloneness. She polished the brass vases and the cluster of altar bells. They tinkled a silvery shower all around her. She refilled the candlesticks with tapering new candles. She breathed in the smell of wax, and the incense that still hovered in the chapel after the previous evening's benediction. It descended around her, enfolding her in a fragrant mist. She moved from pew to pew, dusting, quietly awed. She stopped at each statue to dust its pedestal. She folded her palms and whispered a prayer to each saint. She always thought St Bridget wore the most graceful blue robe, and her smile was the sweetest, but St Anne looked the kindest. Yet there was always something like pathos in their eyes that lessened her pleasure, even as she was drawn to their unearthly beauty. They were so like her mother's eyes in which a similar suffering smouldered. All women were born to suffer through their husbands and sons – her mother said this aloud to anyone who might be listening. It was good, Mala thought, that St Bridget and St Anne remained in their statue selves, or they would end up looking like her mother. Then, she moved to the altar rail. She spread the white cloth over it, preparing it for communion. She knelt to say a decade of the rosary. She knew that her family was in deep need of all her prayers. They had to plead and plead with Jesus, his Holy Mother and all the saints for their daily bread, or they'd starve. That's what her mother said.

When Simon drove the convent car over to the church entrance to drop off a visiting priest to celebrate a special mass, he found Mala at the grotto. Having finished her work, she sat in the sunshine, at the stone entrance, munching the leftover edges of

unblessed host bread and picking flowers off the garlands that had adorned the Mother of Sorrow statue
in the grotto. He would sit by her for a moment perhaps, and she shared her bread with him, her eyes on
a lady in a finely bordered sari, or on the ogling altar
boy in his red and white robes. And she'd ask Simon
for his purse, empty it of last week's remnants, and
reverently place in it, for his new week, a few fresh
flowers that she'd plucked off the garlands. 'God
bless, aiye,' she'd say, returning his purse to him.
Simon took it from her while she leaned back on her
arms, surrendering to the sunshine.

Some fishing seasons were very bad, and the men
drew in nets that held only miserable looking small
fish for the most part. In undertones, they cursed the
big fish that did not cluster to their light, and talked
about demon gods controlling their world. Desperately they'd cast further and further adrift, spending
many extra nights in the sea, the water running out,
the food going bad, and the ice melting in its box.

Then the women stood for hours on the beach
in the dense darkness before dawn, muttering about

the hardships of their lives, terror in every word. The poorest families had just one meal a day, and that was rice and coconut or a bit of dried fish. There was no money even for the cheap keera that Asilin tempered in onion and leftover sprats. Then Mala would run off behind the neighbouring houses and steal their fish drying in the sun. Sometimes she'd return home with her skirt dripping with the dirty kitchen water a woman had thrown at her to drive her away.

And finally, Jamis asked the mudalali to take Priya as a servant to his house. But Asilin was vociferously protective. Priya was too young, she said, and went into a tirade so loud that Jamis growled and swore that they could starve to death for all he cared, and went to try his luck at horses. But he never brought any winnings home. He lost it to the toddy that kept him going in the long unoccupied evenings of the monsoons.

Asilin said, 'Beware of your father when he's after toddy. He turns into a wild animal.'

So the children kept out of his way and played hopscotch in the backyard or wandered up and down the beach with the other children, collecting husks and bramble for firewood, until, their father asleep, they could creep back into the house.

It was on one of these afternoons that Mala and Priya saw their father grab their mother and push her down on the mat. She fell down so heavily that Priya made to rush into the house. But Mala knew better. 'He's drunk and has turned into a wild animal,' she whispered in her mother's voice. They went away. Some time later, they returned, and climbing on a fish box to peer through the window, they saw their mother making a cup of plain tea for their father. As he took it from her, he smiled. They saw her hand lie in his for a moment. It warmed Mala and Priya to see the hands together thus. Then Asilin pulled hers away, walked across to the Mother Mary and Baby Jesus picture in the crevice on the wall, knelt before it, and began to pray. Her lips moved feverishly, and Priya wondered what it was she had suddenly remembered to ask Mother Mary. But Mala knew. Her mother was pleading with Mother Mary to prevent another baby, another mouth to feed. 'Drunken sod,' Mala said to her brother. He nodded wisely. He had implicit trust in his sister, in those days.

Mala and Priya jumped off the fish box. 'When I marry, it will be a rich gentleman from the town side, and he will have a big bed in the house,' Mala said to Priya. Little Priya thought that he himself would never marry anyone, rich or poor. He'd look after his mother and his sister, and all the dogs and cats that had no homes. He would buy his sister all the dresses she wanted, and more. They would never wear the cast-offs any more. He wondered whether he should also look after his twin sisters. But then he'd have to run a fleet of boats, like the mudalali did. All this reminded him to go look for the twins. He found them in the neighbour's garden, playing with each other in the most complicatedly connected way. He felt lonely just looking at them. He returned to trailing Mala.

The mudalali sometimes stopped at their house to collect the boat rent from Jamis. He'd peer into the gloom within, and if he saw Mala, he'd ask their father why he did not send her to work in his house. 'Her mother says she's still too young, mudalali, you know how it is with women,' the father said. Feeling some premonition, Priya would move as close as he could to his sister. But usually she brushed him away as if he were a pestering fly, and stared openly into the mudalali's face. On such an evening, the mudalali would stop by again quite late, with a good-sized fish he'd strung up on a length of string. Mala and Priya would be sitting on the front doorstep staring out at the tourists who walked there, the women running after them trying to sell their wares. Seeing the mudalali approach, Mala would lean backwards on her arms and smile languidly. It seemed to Priya that she smiled differently then, like their father did after a swig of toddy. He hated the way she smiled. He hated the dead round eyes of the fish, and its fixed gaping mouth that suddenly swung so close to his face on the bloodied string.

'Here, I brought some fish for the house. Give this to your mother,' the mudalali said to Mala.

She stood up lazily, even a bit heavily, like an older woman, and took the fish from him. His eyes gleamed over her breasts as she bent to grab the string, and she took her time to turn and saunter back into the house. She returned quite soon and, leaning against the doorpost, she'd sway a bit and giggle. The mudalali would bite the ends of his moustache and walk on. Priya would stare, a fear gnawing at his heart, for he knew not what.

'If you get friendly with the mudalali, Mala akke, you'll have to go and work in his house. So why do you smile with him?' he scolded her. If Simon happened to be visiting, Priya would turn to him for support. Mostly, Simon remained silent.

'And now you'd shout at me too, like everyone else?' Mala said angrily and flounced out of the house towards the sea. Her skirt billowed around her, exposing her legs almost up to her thighs, but she did not care. Priya hoped his mother would not appear at the door and spot her. That would get her in such a state that she'd rush up and drag Mala home by her hair and slap her hard on the cheeks. Priya hated the aftermath of such incidents. They could send Mala into a horrible black mood, and she'd withdraw from everyone. Her silences would fill his world and he'd pray every night to the Mother Mary and Baby Jesus picture until she returned to them. He'd even go to the grotto on Sunday, of his own accord, and light a two-cent candle for her.

'Do you know what I am, Paul? I've worked it all out,' Aruni says. Paul looks up from his book. Aruni's invasions on his space are frequent and sometimes irritating. But he's beginning to look forward to them.

'A coconut,' she says, laughing wildly, 'brown on the outside, white on the inside.'

He gives her his full attention now. There is

something wishful about her tone. When do we finally come to terms with who we are? When we begin to accept all our contradictions? When we stop searching for the core? When we take ourselves for granted because we have never had to prove ourselves? Why was it all so important? He has never tried to define himself.

He tells her to sit down. But no, she says she has other things to do. He sees her at the far end of the pool, a while later, playing ball with some tourists. There is one Frenchman in particular who tries to chat her up. He places a flower on her plate every night when they sit down to dinner in the dining room. 'Fleur pour la petite fleur,' he says to her with a flourish, winking with Paul. She touches the flower in many moods and Paul, watching her, is glad to be there – a protective presence.

He turns back to his book but is still caught up in Aruni's self-definition. He knows that in Australia it is nothing if not pejorative. But even here, in her motherland, she is neither tourist nor local. The villagers address her as missy – that is endearing. But Paul has heard the beach boys, with whom she so passionately claims kinship, surreptitiously call her kalu suddhi – she's heard it too. It means black-white woman, she translates for him nonchalantly. But that's not me, Paul, she insists – I'm a local, see? This is my country. I belong here. Belonging, so important to her. And she has belonged nowhere so far, she says. No mother, no home, no country.

But what about in Australia? Isn't that home? he asks. Oh, always the alien there, she says. She laughs but her eyes are congested with unhappiness. Cleaving eyes, needy eyes. You want to lean forward and wipe them clear. They'd shifted around a lot, she says – from Brisbane to Sydney to Adelaide to Melbourne, all in ten years. Her father could not get a job to match his qualifications. So they migrated from state to state, hoping to strike gold somewhere. Aruni – eternally the new kid in school. She got used to it after years, she'd bury herself in a book – Aruni, the quiet clever girl. At home, her parents had their own secret to guard. Friends were dropped overnight, if they touched on the personal. And the silence that hung over her family, like a fog hiding each from the other – it was enough to drive us all nuts, she says. When she returns to Oz, if she returns, having untangled herself by then, she'll live alone. But why go to Australia, she says again, why not stay on here? In my country, with my people? Paul can't make out whether she's serious or not. But he carries her hurt with him for some time.

In the meantime, the waiters call her nothing at all, having decided she and Paul are having an affair – and that seems equally insulting to Paul. When she is not with him, the other hotel guests refer to her as 'his woman'. How's that woman of yours, mate? Ripe mango, what? Paul responds with a long-suffering smile.

And then almost overnight Mala was all grown up. No one could say she was only fifteen. Their mother began to keep a constant look out for her, advise her endlessly about how she should behave, how she should not do this or that with the beach boys. She made Mala wear a cloth around her short skirts, even in the house. She made her kneel at her side in the late evenings to recite the family rosary. Mala would retort that she prayed better while dusting the statues and polishing the brass in the chapel. When Asilin forced her with a shove or two, Mala went down on her knees but would stubbornly refuse to respond to the Hail Marys. She'd play with the rosary beads, holding them against the flame of the lamp before the Mother Mary and Baby Jesus picture and stare into their glowing red depths. Priya could see two tiny red lamps in her black eyes – maybe, he thought, God was turning her into a kinduri and growing her a fish tail. Kneeling by her, he quailed for his sister. He expected the rosary to turn into a snake because she was using it for something other than prayer. Sometimes, she stood up boldly and went out to roam the beaches. Then Priya would be sent to look for her. Often, he stopped at Simon's house and made inquiries. Buttoning up his shirt, and taking his torch, Simon joined Priya in the search.

It was on one of these twilights that Simon and Priya saw Mala smiling in her wayward way with a white man. Priya stopped walking and stared. In stunned silence he glanced back, expecting their mother to run up with the stick to drive Mala back home. Was Mala akka deaf? Had she not heard their mother rant on and on about the consequences of getting caught in the suddha's net? Had they not been threatened with all kinds of fearful punishments if she ever caught them with the white men on the beach? Didn't she say that that was the first step, before they were lured into the tourist hotels and cabanas far

down? But here was Mala, in spite of all that, swaying her body with that secret rhythm that glued men's
eyes to her body. Any moment now, she might fall
into his arms, the way she was going, so bold.

But it didn't get to that, not on the beach. The
man said something to Mala and began to walk away.
Mala turned round once, and perhaps saw them in
the distance. But then, she began to walk jauntily
behind the man towards the tourist hotels, past the
cabanas. The man did not once turn towards her, or
take her hand or anything nice like that. Maybe this
was about something else altogether, Priya thought,
beginning to trail them.

'Let's go back, Mala will be home later,' Simon
called out to Priya. But Priya shook his head and continued to walk on. Simon turned towards his own
house. He kept glancing back, hoping that Priya
would follow him. He noticed, with a hollow feeling,
the way the waves washed over the sand where their
footprints changed direction. Once home, Simon
leaned against a pillar on his verandah and waited for
some time for the children to return. Then he lit up
a cigarette, and went into town.

After two hours of loitering by the hotel fence,
Priya felt lost. He was hungry too, and finally, he

walked around the fence and reached the formal hotel entrance from the main road. He watched the fountain play in the open courtyard, but soon, the bellhop chased him away.

'Malli, are you trying to catch a suddha? This is not the place. Go to the beach,' he said not unkindly. One or two of the taxi drivers beckoned to him. Priya ran away without a word.

He crept into the house. No one was home, and he slid open the door for himself. He wandered around in the semi-darkness, looked into empty cooking pots, and then remembered that their mother had gone off to the village to sell a good catch of fish. This meant that they'd have a late dinner when she returned with the vegetables she bought after selling the fish. He sat on the back step to wait for her. He sighed with his chin in his palm. His father would be at the bookie shop gambling on those horses that never won a race. Their mother said bitterly that the horses that the father bet on, rushed up to the winning line, then without crossing it, turned and ran the other way. No one protested against the father's gambling, though, because when he was around, they had all to stay out of his way. He'd either be snoring in the camp-bed on the verandah and they'd have to tiptoe around the house, or if awake, yelling at one of them to run errands for him. If he saw Priya now, he'd order him off to mend the nets or catch a few basket fish in the lagoon, or make him a glass of plain tea. Priya was sick of making tea for everyone in his family, but he did it anyway, without protest. Now, he wished he'd gone with his mother. She might even have bought him a toy or some tissue paper for a kite, if she sold all the fish.

Priya loved going with his mother to the rich people's houses in the town. As they approached each gate, he'd jump up and shoot back the latch, and open the gate wide so his mother did not have to pause with the heavy basket balanced on top of her head. She'd sail in if the basket was full, singing tunefully, 'malu, malu, muhudu malu.' Often the mistress of the house would be waiting for her on the threshold, and a servant, sometimes two, would help her lower the basket to the polished cement floor.

Priya would squat on the step beside the basket. Freed of it, and of the reed ring on which she placed it, his mother would unfold her konde, pull back her hair and tie it up tightly again. Priya helped out by getting out the clanging scales, arranging the weights in a pyramid shape, and shooing away the crows that gathered for the pickings. Sitting on the step and wiping her massive knife, Asilin would then begin the long process of bargaining, and weighing, and cutting the fish. Often, the lady of the house complained about the sand thrown in with the fish. Or, if too many flies settled on the basket, she raised the fish's fin to check its freshness, and press at its flesh. Asilin then hurriedly compromised, wiping some of the sand from the fish and swearing that it had been caught that very morning. Not like the fish they sold in the fish shop, she continued. But the lady of the house refused to accept this argument. Priya and his mother left such a house disgruntled. Asilin cursed the mistress and her rich household, making sure her voice was low enough not to endanger her sales forever, while Priya, if no one was looking, would leave the gate ajar so stray dogs could get in. He hoped one of them would bite the legs off the fat spoilt housedog that took a snipe at his ankle whenever it could.

Invariably they stopped at the mudalali's house. But this was not to sell fish, because the mudalali always bought their best fish anyway. The mudalali's wife would offer them two glasses of plain tea loaded with sugar. Priya's mouth watered even before he saw the glasses. The mudalali's wife sat in a deep chair in the polished verandah, and listened to all the gossip that Priya's mother had gleaned in the village. They exchanged views about why some woman had jumped into the well, or why Paulus had chopped his wife into pieces the week before. Priya knew why they talked this way. His mother said that the mudalali's wife had been a beach girl herself, before she had the good fortune to marry the mudalali. She had not always been so finely dressed, or so grand a lady of a house, Asilin said, with the hint of a sneer. That was one reason she refused to send Priya to work in this house. The more obvious reason she gave was that the family status in the village would sink to zero if the children had to work as servants. Priya could not understand the logic behind any of this, but as long as it kept him out of the servant population, he did not worry. With his mouth open, he gazed at the mudalali's wife, wondering if Mala would catch a fish as big as the mudalali and live in a big house like this. He knew his mother hoped in her secret heart.

'This child is always gaping with his mouth open – is he trying to catch flies?' the mudalalis's wife said. She gave him a bulto to plug up his mouth, and he sucked it all the way back home.

After such a visit, Priya walked happily beside his mother. He did not have to leap ahead, as with Mala, because Asilin walked slowly and rhythmically, balancing the basket and slowing down at each gate. If she was in a good mood, with the basket emptying, and the money purse fat between her breasts, she gave him a few cents to buy a scoop of ice-cream-on-a-wafer from the ice-cream bicycle in the market.

One time he bought a spinning top. He still has it, Simon says. It was a funny shape, like two small cones glued together in the middle. With a quick flick of his fingers, he could make it spin round and round on the cemented surface of Simon's verandah. It excited all the small boys of the village. Painted in horizontal stripes of red and blue and yellow, the top became a kaleidoscope when it spun, making Priya's head dizzy with colour. Some day, Simon told him, just once in a lifetime, the top could be made to spin even on soft dry sand. When this happened, Simon said, you'd know your time was right, and then all prosperity would be yours.

Though Priya was not taken in by this, there were moments when he ran to the beach with his top and tried to spin it. But it just tipped sideways on to the sand without a single spin. Once, when his family was close to starving, Priya dreamt that he spun the top in the beach and that it danced round madly. Hundreds of multicoloured fish jumped out of its tip. He and Mala and their mother and father together couldn't catch them all, there were so many. And they clutched each other, and rolled on the sand, laughing. He awakened hungrier than ever. He crawled on to his sister's mat and she cuddled him against her. He'd not taken the top out of his tin box for days after that.

Now, sitting on the back step with his glass of lukewarm tea, worrying about Mala and how she'd gone off with the white man, who knew where, Priya wished he'd accompanied his mother and her fish basket that day. He drank the bitter tea in small gulps. There was not a grain of sugar or piece of juggery in the house. He peered at a trail of black ants swiftly carrying their white eggs around the edge of the step. That's a good omen, his mother would say, and make him step over it for luck. He stood up and stepped over it, back and forth, back and forth. But he sat down again, sighing. It would take more than a million black ants with white eggs to bring them luck.

And then he saw his mother ambling down the road. Splashing out the tea dregs on the sand, he ran up to her. She smiled as he clung to her cloth. He was comforted by her sweaty fish-smell and drew even closer, until she shoved him away with a swing of her hips.

'Always clinging on to a woman's cloth,' she scolded. 'When are you going to stand alone, boy?' But there was no irritation in her voice, just a rough affection. Priya sniffled more confidently by her.

He helped her lower the basket and peered in. It was thinly layered with vegetables and a ripe mango or two peeped incredibly out of the green leaf, the bright red tomato, and the deep orange roots of the bathala. He knew then that she'd had a lucky day.

'That mango for me, amme?' asked Priya, the spit collecting on his lips.

'That's for you and Mala, the other one is for the sisters. Don't touch it,' she replied, giving him one.

'But they eat mango pickle after school, amme. Prancina Hamy buys it for them,' Priya protested.

But Asilin spoke no more. Wearily, she sat down on the step, and asked him to prepare a glass of tea for her, and then go next door to collect the twins. Priya set about blowing into the fire and making sure there was water in the kettle. He then brought out to his mother the bottle of coconut oil. She held the bottle to her nose, sniffed it, held it to the light to see how much oil it contained. She poured just a drop or two into her palm and began to rub it into her head. 'It seems like I've been carrying a lorry, child,' she grumbled. Priya looked at her miserably. He decided to leave the story of Mala and the white man for later.

Asilin sighed and stretched out her legs. Squatting before her, Priya began to massage her feet. They were dusty from so much walking, the soles cracked wide and dry. He drained the bottle for the last drop of oil, knocking its mouth hard against his palm to force it out. He applied it to the cracks. Asilin closed her eyes and leaned against the door-frame. He wanted to rest his head in her lap and spill out his hurt about Mala but not a word escaped his lips. When he heard the water boiling, he returned to the kitchen. He poured the tea, and cut the mango. Leaving one half on a plate for his sister, he sliced the other half off the seed. He took it to his mother with the glass of tea.

Sitting by her, he began to suck the seed. The juice dripped from his mouth and he curled out his tongue to get it back. But he could not taste the full sweetness because his head was in turmoil. Should he tell his mother what he had seen? But that would send her into such a fit, he knew, and spoil this quiet moment. Later, he thought, he'd think about what should be done, later. He wiped his lips and went off to get the twins.

Priya never told on Mala. Even now, Simon says to Aruni, on those rare occasions when he steps out of his stupor, Priya wonders about it. Could it have made a difference, he would ask Simon, had he sneaked about Mala to his mother in those early days? Could it have altered the history of their family? Could Mala have been saved? Could Mala's daughter have had another life – not over there in Australia but here, in her own village, with her own people? Neither Simon nor Priya had any answers. Asilin, after cursing everything and everyone in her life throughout the day, would say at the end of it, that what happened usually happened because God willed it so. She would then light the wick before the Mary and Jesus picture.

It was around this time that Priya stopped questioning God about why He willed such tragedy on his family. His mother would have slapped him hard had she known his thoughts. Once, when he was a bit younger, he had asked Father at confession why God created rich people and poor people. Father was silent for a bit and Priya gazed uneasily into the confessional, trying to guess Father's reaction. But Father's voice was soothing soft when he told Priya that his aim in life was not to question God, but to do as He wished. The very next day, Father appeared at their doorstep with a parcel of second-hand clothes that had arrived from the Federation students in Colombo.

Hiding behind the door, Priya wished he had not asked that question in the confessional. He felt he had betrayed his family's secrets to a stranger. But his mother had been so pleased, blessing Father over and over again. 'May God bless you, Father, may God bless you,' she whispered, looking at the package as if she held gold in her hands.

Father had never let on about Priya and the confession. And that had been the beginning of the Church's relationship with his family. Anyway, questions led nowhere. As Father had said, it was wiser to go about doing what had to be done. But Priya was so grateful to Father that he would sniffle behind him on his rounds in the village. He'd dream that when he got rich, he'd present Father with a bicycle so he did not have to tread on the filth lying around the shanties.

Even in those days, when he was not required to drive the convent car, Simon sold kurumba on the beach. He still likes the beach best when it is tranquil, he says. He draws his chair out into the sand, heaps up the green nuts at his side. He likes to read and compose small verses that he scratches into an old exercise book. He looks around at the beach boys whose voices break now and then into high pitch, shouting to each other about the white men, and what they gleaned from them.

It had been no different in those long-ago days. There had been more boys then, of course, Simon says, because the village was much larger. Little by little it shrank, especially when the dinghies began to replace the catamarans in the bigger villages. Some of the families less in debt to the mudalali migrated to try their hands at fishing with the dinghies. Most of them never came back. Then the Japanese started drag net fishing. They trapped the fish in the high seas, leaving little for our men who fished in the mid sea.

So even in those days, the beach boys lived off the tourists. They learned their trade from one another, and by fourteen and fifteen, they knew all there was to know about drugs, prostitution, pimping and God knows what else. The stray dogs trailed them, and sometimes, a younger boy or two, like Priya. When he saw Simon, Priya stopped following the gang, and settled down on his haunches by Simon's chair. Simon offered him a sip of kurumba, and refreshed, Priya would begin to sketch on the sand. Sometimes, he erased a letter that Priya had drawn back to front, and guided Priya's finger to write it correctly. But as soon as he let go, Priya went back to drawing the letter back to front. Simon returned to his book, but often his eyes lingered on the boy. He'd ask Priya some trivial thing, so that Priya turned his luminous large eyes on him. Eyes like deep pools lit from within.

One day, Mala appeared as from nowhere, and began to jiggle her bright new bangles and show off her new slippers. Twisting her head sideways, she showed them her new butterfly hair slides. She told Simon that she had got them from the Sisters, and that next week, she'd buy those other slides that were shaped like flowers. She chattered on and on. But Priya leaned forward and whispered to Simon that Mala got her spending money from the white men. 'Tell her not to do such things, Simon aiye,' he whispered in Simon's ear. But Simon pretended not to hear him. She was growing up with so little. He felt in his belt-purse and offered her five rupees.

'Buy the flower slides tomorrow, or they may get sold,' he said to her. It saddened him to see how eagerly she took the money and hid it in her blouse like a grown woman.

Soon, the beach boys and even some of the older men began to hang around Mala. Simon and Priya watched as Mala learned to flirt back with them. She grew bold and knowing. She bought slinky dresses with the money that she always seemed to have these days. There she was in the twilight, a flash of red, leaning against this tree or that, by the sea, or along the beach, with a group of men, or Rathu or any of his friends. Now the village gossiped about Mala all the time. It made Priya blush when even the smaller boys began to joke about his sister. They said everybody knew Mala was a free-for-all – a basketball that could be shoved from hand to hand.

At the beginning, Priya tried to stick up for his sister. But as time went on, and the gossips got more strident, he slunk away and hid from them. He became even lonelier than before. He'd often sit on the beach and daydream, and the beach got used to him being this way, some even said his mind was vacant and that he was just a good-for-nothing. He grew so thin and pale, he looked transparent.

'What are you thinking about, aiye?' Simon looked up astonished one early morning. Mala stood close by his chair, almost touching him. Her face was fresh and clean as if she had just returned from her bath at the road tap. Still only half awake, he gazed right up into her eyes. She smiled back, but then, unable to hold his unfamiliarly intimate gaze, she cast down her eyes. Her smile faded. But it had sparked in Simon a lovely flame. He let it burn secretively.

'I couldn't sleep. It's too hot. Want some kurumba?' he asked, bending in confusion. What was she doing here at this time of morning? It was barely even dawn, and the catamarans still a fair distance away from the shore. Not a man or woman in sight.

'No, I've just had some milk tea,' Mala said in a strange shrill voice, 'with a white gentleman in the hotel.'

She looked at him boldly, straightening up to her full height as if to defend herself against his anger. But he only sat back in his chair, and when he looked at her face again, it was with resignation. Who was he to judge her? She was a flower smothered in a dung heap, seeking light.

'I didn't go home last night,' she continued, a tremor in her voice.

When he still said nothing, her body crumpled, and with a sigh, she squatted beside his chair.

Simon wondered what he should say. She should be at Father Lucien's confessional. Father would know what to say to her. He studied her face, and knew it was not poverty alone that lured her to the white men. He wished she were not so sensual. That she could be free of this need, so she could be free of the men who were going to abuse her, one after another, and then drive her onto the streets. But even as he thought this, he could not control his hand moving up to caress her cheek. The eyes stared back into his, no longer those of the child he knew. His eyes shifted down to her body. She wore her red dress and she had wrapped over it a colourful batik cloth to keep out the chill of dawn.

He would remember always, even when he thought all feeling for her had drained away, that the cloth had a pattern of fruit on it, pineapples and mangoes, and that it seemed to be held up at the neck by a garland of flowers. And how the face, now close to him, seemed aglow still, how it seemed to hold the ecstasy of last night's moonlight. He traced the line of her lips with his fingers. He sensed tears just below the surface of her eyes.

'Does your mother know about this? Or Priya or anyone?' he asked gently.

But his mind was also caught within its own secrets. He felt, with a kind of shock, the physical stirring that was unexpected and unwelcome. Desire for contact with her brushed against him. There was about her the fragrance of hotel soap. Drops of water still dripped from her hair and, without conscious thought, Simon circled the ends of the long strands around his fingers and drained the water from them. She responded as if this intimacy had always happened, the most natural thing in the world. She bent towards him, and his fingers moved reluctantly along her neck. He did not know, he would think again and again through the years, whether he was awake or dreaming.

'What do you want now, my Mala?' Even as he said the words he realised that he had spoken to her in the only way he knew, as if she were still a child entreating him for something – begging him to carry her to the sea, take her for a ride in the convent car, dye coconut refuse to pave the church road with flower mosaics for Corpus Christi.

'Will you marry me, aiye?' she said simply, with a half smile, but there was fear lurking somewhere in her.

'Marry you?' he repeated stupidly. 'You want me to marry you?' There was nothing before and beyond, but the woman who bent to him. Like a splendid flower she began to blossom in his heart. 'Why?' he asked. Did she love him then, in spite of all those men she went with? Could she be saved by him from what was to be? Could he be saved by her? It was a dream that he had not had the courage to dream.

'I will tell you, aiye. And it is the truth, I swear. I have never lied to you. I want to be your woman, and look after the house, and have your child.'

The blossom withered. A child. She wanted him to protect her, give his name to a child. Simon withdrew. He felt a dull, sorrowful anger for her, for the unborn child. And overriding all, an immense relief. Her voice crooned now. The words sounded practised, honey-sweet, dripping off the tongue of an actress. He saw her face as he had seen it last night when she'd sauntered past his house towards the hotel – the smudged lipstick, the eyes darkened with charcoal, the cheeks cheaply rouged.

'But you have just been with a white gentleman,' he said, seeking time. 'What shall we do about him?'

'Let him rot in the sea,' Mala returned violently. 'They are all the same, all the same, no different. All like animals, like my father when he is drunk.'

Simon felt the bond between them stretch and stretch into an ache, a suffocating tightness. He wanted her to go away, go away and leave him to return to himself. He preferred the dream of her.

'I don't think I can marry you, Mala,' he said. But he was helpless against the void that was opening up in him.

'But why not?' she asked incredulously. She

was again the innocent little thing who bent him imperiously to her will. Mala – the centre of her little world, and always so strongly on the periphery of his.

Why had it all to change? And now, there was Priya.

'Come with me into the house,' Simon said to her at last, pulled in too many directions. Her eyes gleamed with hope. 'I will make you a cup of tea,' he continued and watched the hope die. He turned and took her hand as they walked. She followed him as if it was all she had ever desired.

She stood just behind him in the narrow space of his kitchen as he stirred two heaped spoons of sugar into her tea, the way she liked it. His body brushed against hers as he turned to give it to her. She received the glass with a humble gesture, in both hands. 'Simon aiye, forgive me,' she whispered. She placed her cup, the tea untasted, on the table behind him. With this gesture she moved closer. He could feel her breath on his neck. It was almost as if she lay against him, and he'd put his arms around her. Simon remembers the limpid beauty of the moment.

She looked up at him imploringly. Mutely.

'I can't,' he said stepping aside. 'I am sorry, Mala, there are reasons.' But he cupped her face in his palms. 'Let me look at you – from a small distance like this. I love to look at you. That's all I've ever wanted. Don't you know that?'

She stood silent and still. It seemed to him that she was resting, like a boat adrift between storms. And then she withdrew, little by little, into herself, and away. He felt bereft. His hands fell away from her face.

'This is about Priya malli, isn't it?' she asked with cruelly narrowed eyes, leaning back and widening the distance between them. And now he could only stare at her incredulously. He shrank from the fear of being discovered. 'I am not a child, Simon aiye, I know about you and Priya.' Simon could only gaze at her in anguished astonishment. Suddenly exposed, overcome with hurt, he raised his palm to shield his eyes from her, from the world.

Mala backed out of the kitchen and walked away. Simon went out into the verandah and watched until she turned into her own house. He lay down on the bed on the verandah. He stared up at the rafters. He closed his eyes on Mala. But Priya? He wanted only to be alone, to hide his secret desire, destroy it, and bury it. But he knew he would fail. Mala's words had driven dreams and nightmares into reality. If only life could be lived from a distance, he thought. Gradually, as always in a crisis, Simon entered that place of deep calm within himself. It closed around him, and walled out his external world.

But how dismal his small house, now she had gone away. Will we meet again, here at your flowering grave, two white birds? He yearned for her sounds in his kitchen, her gossip, and the tenderness with which she tempted him to taste just a little more of the jadi she'd brought him, or the dried fish that she had tempered in onion, just the way he liked it.

Gradually, the beach lost Mala to the white men. She stayed away more and more during the day, and even in the evenings and late into the nights. At first, Asilin berated her when she returned home, and even slapped her once or twice and threatened to tell Jamis. But she unfailingly waited for Mala, sitting on the front doorstep, her chin in her hand. Often, late at night, stepping past her mother, Mala would hold out a five-rupee note. With a big lump in his heart, Priya watched his mother's worn fingers close over it. He saw the way she avoided meeting Mala's eyes. Wearily she'd reach up and put the note in the broken-handled cup that she kept hidden behind the Mother Mary and Baby Jesus picture. Gossiping friends hinted to Jamis about his daughter's doings. But when he tried to question her, Asilin somehow changed the subject to how he was wasting all their money drinking and gambling. If not for the money that the girl and I bring in, you'd be sleeping in an ambalama like a beggar, she said. He would then turn violent, swear he'd kill her if she didn't shut up, and storm off to sleep in the verandah.

Simon was sitting on his verandah on one of these nights when he heard Priya shouting to him in a terrified voice. Switching on his torch, and folding his sarong up to his knees, he stepped out quickly. Priya clutched at his arm and rushed him towards the road.

'It's our Mala, Simon aiye, they are hooting at her all down the road. You have to do something. Come, aiye, come quickly.'

And even as they ran across the railway line to the main road, he saw Mala walking stiffly towards them as a stream of insults was hurled at her by the butik men on either side of the road. 'Go back to the white men, vesi, you won't find what you want among the likes of us any more.' They flashed their torches at parts of her body, and they gleamed in slivers. Simon pressed Priya against his waist, trying to shield him from hearing and seeing.

'Do something, aiye, God bless you, do something.'

But Simon only held Priya closer to him. Mala asked for no help from anyone. She just kept walking, straight and sure. The men yelled even louder to the rhythm of her body, and one or two jumped out on the road, their sarongs tucked up around their thighs. They began to sing boisterously, a drunken baila about a woman who stood behind her half-opened door enticing men to her. 'Open the door, my Mala, open the door for us,' they sang, their laughter shredding the night's peacefulness. It was then that Priya escaped Simon's grip, and rushed to Mala, reaching for her hand. She took it and continued walking. She walked right past Simon, as if she had not seen him, and turned to her house at the far end.

Aruni could no longer be silent. 'Did you do anything, Simon? The people respected you, surely you could have stopped them?'

'No, missy, I did not do anything,' Simon says,

'Who can say how we react in a crisis? And may God curse me for it. We all had a hand in the way things turned out for your mother.'

A few nights later, neighbours slung buckets of excrement on the front door of Jamis' house. Asilin spent hours scrubbing the door clean, but the smell clung to the house for months. When Mala slunk in reeking with perfume, Asilin yelled at her to go back where she'd come from. Jamis swore at them all, and demanded to know where she had been. She stood against the doorway then, sullen and unhappy, and silent. And then Jamis got more and more angry, and lunged at her and pummelled her. She fell against the wall and slid down weeping to the door.

'Bitch,' he yelled, 'you have smeared our name in the shit of the pariah dogs.'

Then Mala came alive, and swore back at them all, standing proud and alone, cursing them in words that they had never heard her use, blaming them all for her fate. Suddenly seeing the slight protrusion of her belly, Priya shrank against the wall.

'You dare accuse me of smearing our name?'

she screamed at her father, her hands at her hips. 'I've seen you, you filthy pig. I've seen you with Seela and Maggie and all those other women, drunk, fiddling with them in the huts . . . Don't think I've not heard the gossip.' She turned to her mother. 'And how many times have you taken the money that I brought home from the suddhas? It was good enough to keep all the family from starving, wasn't it? Everyone in the house knows where the money comes from.'

Priya cringed. He saw his father's eyes dilate with fury and moved as close as he could to his mother. He felt her shudder against him, and stared into her face. He saw it crumbling, crumbling, the vestiges of beauty vanishing forever.

But Mala would not be silenced. She screamed, 'And what do you want from *me* when you're drunk? Think I don't know? I've seen it in your eyes, you drunken sod. Oh, you are a wild animal when you are drunk.'

The family stared, speechless. But it was all too much for Mala. Suddenly, she collapsed at her father's feet and crouched. Then, dragging herself up, she twisted her arms around his legs and looked up beseechingly. Nonplussed, Jamis gazed down at her. A shroud of silence fell around them. The family cowered in suspense. Priya saw his mother glance at the holy picture in the crevice in the wall. He saw the way the wick drooped in the lamp. He fell down on his knees before the picture and the unlit wick, and folded his palms. A prayer dribbled hysterically from his lips.

But it was no good. Jamis pulled his legs away from his daughter's clutch. He thrust away her begging hands. She lay crushed and weeping on the floor. Without warning, he bent down, grabbed her by the hair and dragged her to the verandah. Asilin rushed up and tried to pull them apart. But the father's rage spilled over, cursing them all. And in a gesture of hopeless love, or hate, he pulled Mala up close against him. And then, even as she tried to wrap her arms tiredly around him, he flung her back. She fell against the doorpost. She clung to it and tried to crawl back in to the house. He kicked her until she fell out into the beach.

'Go and have your pariah somewhere else, don't litter this house with it, you bitch, you daughter of a bitch,' he shouted.

At last, Mala lay inert. In the stillness that followed, there was only Priya's prayerful voice squeaking on and on.

Ignoring everyone, Jamis pulled the fishing gear

from the rafter and, slinging it over his shoulder, stepped into the garden. Asilin, suddenly activated, took the kerosene oil lamp with the long spout, and ran after him.

'Here, children's father,' she shouted over the rush of waves, 'take the lamp, you forgot the lamp.'

Jamis stopped and stretched out his arm for it. But she had not yet filled it with oil. He took it anyway and she turned aside. She had cleaned and filled that lamp without fail all these years, to light up his nights. Now it hung from his hand, empty and useless. He began to walk towards the boat.

Asilin turned back to the house. But neighbours were standing around it in twos and threes, peering in. A few were bent over Mala. Asilin raised her hands as if to smooth and knot back her hair before going to them. But her hands could only clutch the back of her head. Her body arched backwards and there rose from its depths wail after agonized wail. She raised a begging face to the sky as if it would split open a sacred river to wash away the sorrow and the humiliation.

She began to run, like a woman insane, into the night. Her lips blubbered as if they had a life all their own. Mother Mary please protect us. Mother Mary have mercy on us. Mother Mary ask your holy son

Jesus to save us. Aiyo, save us from this disaster . . . She rushed down the beach. Now and then, a woman or child hailed her. But Asilin heard nothing, saw no one. She ended up at the line of hotels. She fell against the fence and pushed and rattled its iron bars, cursing the white men inside who had sucked out her daughter's body and then thrown back the refuse.

Two security guards stood by. They regarded her from beneath the hoods of black coats, and she saw them malevolent, like hooded birds of prey. 'Have you come to look for our Mala?' one asked. 'We've not seen her today.' She crept closer then, as if they offered her shelter. She thought she detected kindness in the voice. But they leered with the memory of Mala, and made obscene gestures as if they held her body between them. Asilin fell back from the fence. She wandered around blindly, like an animal searching for its lost litter.

Dawn was breaking when she returned home. On the way, she passed Simon sitting under the tree, regarding the sea-drenched beach. When he called to her she paused, as if returning from some far-away lonely place.

'Aney Simon,' she moaned, 'we are in such trouble.' She poured out her story. He listened and saw how she had aged in the last few hours. 'Please, Simon, will you advise our Mala to be a good girl? She is lost to us.'

He led her into his house and made her a cup of tea. She swallowed it in loud gulps. Simon said he would tell the convent sisters to help Mala. Asilin seemed comforted, somewhat. 'Jesu pihitai,' she blessed him.

Priya shifts against the tree. He gazes uneasily at Aruni. Her shoulders gleam with sweat and sun, and her beach cloth lies loosely around her breasts. There is about her face a kind of recklessness, a bold curiosity. She is an unwelcome presence, always. But when she asks her questions and refuses to go away, he senses her loneliness. He is all burnt out, but now and then, in her presence, a memory sparks. And then he remembers that she resembles his sister. Mala. Her spirit walks in his midnight sleep. He wakes up and can't work out the centre of his dream – he can only clutch at loose ends. He walks the beach seeking her. He rolls another cigarette, and then he sees her in the distance, her red skirt fluttering in the breeze. He runs to meet her, his arms opening wide.

Priya was eleven years old. He was sitting idle on the beach staring into the sea. He was hungry and this restricted his movements. He wore his one pair of shorts. His skinny chest was bare, as always.

Then, there was someone else. An old white man. A tourist, his skin burnt red in the sun. He wore a skimpy pair of bathers and a shining silver watch. Priya was still unaware of his presence. He had tried to draw on the wet sand, a letter or two remembered from his few sporadic terms in school. The letters were unformed and would soon be erased from sand and memory. Waves smashed against rock. The sun was a searing eye in the cloudless sky. Priya was small and unprotected on the shore. And hungry.

He was used to tourists of course. They were part of their lives after all. Mala now had a half-white-half-brown baby that lay on a threadbare mat in a corner of the hut. Its father was unknown. Mala had revealed nothing, not even after their father beat her up and kicked her out of the house. Everyone was ashamed of it, even Priya. Some of the boys understood, however. He was not the only one in such a situation. The half-caste was over two months old now. But it had no name. Priya's mother was waiting for it to die, everyone knew that. It was undernourished and would whimper the day away on the mat until she yelled at him to throw the pariah in the sea. He would be careful not to take it out of the hut where a neighbour woman could see it and comment about its birth and cast insults about his sister's character. Occasionally, hurt by the wrinkled red face and sad sunken eyes, Priya would put his finger in its searching mouth and let it suck suck suck. He longed for Mala to return home. But she had run away leaving no trace.

He missed Mala. He could see her now, in her clinging red dress, returning home late after their father had sailed away to sea. Sometimes she brought him a bulto from the tea butik. She would swing him off the ground and swirl him round and round until, tangled in the long tresses of her hair and the red folds of her skirt, they would fall, laughing, in a heap on the soft sand. When she was in a good humour, and there was a lull in the wind, she would call him behind the house, mix a bit of soap in water, dip a pawpaw stem in it and blow rainbow bubbles for him. In the chilly nights he curled into her warmth, and though she grumbled a bit, she covered him with her cloth. But now she was gone. Their mother cursed the day Mala had been born and said she would burn forever in hell. But Priya knew she reserved a decade in her rosary for Mala. The hurt of Mala stung Priya's heart.

The old white man greeted Priya. Startled out of his reflections, Priya stared at him blankly. The man gauged the thin body, and he almost moved away. But for his liquid eyes, the child was not attractive. Then again, neither was he. He hesitated to approach the bigger boys or the pimps because they might make fun of his sagging body, his age. The watch glinted brilliantly in Priya's eyes. Had he been bigger and stronger, he might have grabbed it and run. It would have fed his family for a week.

'Where do you live?' the man asked and Priya pointed. Even as they watched, his mother came out of the house in a rush, turned some bits of salted fish drying in the sun, tightened her cloth around her waist, and went in. Had she seen him, she would have called to him. But she was busy and had no time to look.

The man surveyed the scene: fishermen rested here and there against the catamarans dragged onshore after their night at sea. Many of them were bleary eyed with toddy. A mangy dog slunk about in search of scraps and was sometimes kicked. Now and then, someone picked up a strand of baila. But it hardly caught on.

For the majority, the night had been unsuccessful and there was a sense of tiredness, of defeated will. After the mudalali claimed his share of the meagre haul, often there was nothing at all to sell. Just a few undersized fish that the women would cook for the family later in the afternoon. At this time of mid-morning, a few of the luckier women were returning home with empty baskets after quick sales, others tended their children, wound husk into coir, or just sat around picking lice and gossiping. The old white man dismissed them contemptuously and turned back to the boy.

'Want to come with me? I have chocolates

and cigarettes,' he said in English. Priya understood chocolates and cigarettes. He also had a vague idea about why the man offered them to him. A number of the boys he hung around with smoked foreign cigarettes, traded foreign chocolates and chewing gum, and wore shiny nylon shirts and shiny watches. They also made subtle jokes about how they came about such goodies. Priya's mother was aware of these goings on. She threatened him daily. She swore she would burn his legs or beat him until he could never walk again if she found him in a suddha's net. 'Do you hear me?' she asked him, tweaking his ear, after such a tirade. 'Yes, amme,' he said to her each time. At night, when she was not too tired, she would make him kneel with the twins by the Mary and Jesus picture. When she had oil in the house she carefully measured out a lid-full into the small glass bowl that sat in front of the picture, and lit the wick. The dim flame would light up the red of Mother Mary's cheeks, her tranquil lips and the gold-dusted skin of the baby Jesus. Sleepily Priya would stare at the picture and think to himself that the baby Jesus was a plumped up, dimpled version of their Mala's baby. Often, before his mother finished her rosary, Priya would curl up on the floor at her feet. At last, she would bend down to lift him up and lay him a few feet away by the baby. Then Priya wrapped his arms around her neck and gazed at her with eyes that held dreams. He was the baby Jesus who suffused her face with Mary's glow.

Now, Priya looked back towards the hut in a panic. He'd had nothing but plain tea since morning. His hunger would grow with the day, and when he returned home at dinner time, his mother would ask him why he could not earn some money by mending a net or repairing a boat. She never meant what she said and usually doled out a spoonful of rice for him with a bit of fish curry or shredded coconut. She knew he was too weak and timid for anything but school. He could not even sell a shell or a garland of beads to a tourist without a bigger boy cuffing him on the head and grabbing the money from him. But who could afford the books and the clothes needed for school? The church helped but that was hardly sufficient. His father said he should be employed as a servant in the mudalali's big house. After Mala's scandal, the good sisters had found a place for Priya's twin sisters. That was bad enough, and his mother cringed with shame when she had to speak of it. Whenever she dwelt on Priya in the mudalali's bungalow, however, her blood ran cold. Everyone knew the mudalali was a shark. So she postponed the decision.

Priya craved for the chocolates that the bigger boys munched in front of his eyes in the evenings. After Mala disappeared, he trailed them obsessively. Occasionally, they remembered to throw him a titbit that he tossed down without even tasting. Now the old white man looked at the skinny child, at his naked chest and narrow hips from which his shorts, several sizes too large for him hung down. His eyes blurred and his lips thickened lasciviously. He pointed to his watch and held it out. He began to walk away. He knew the boy had little choice, and that he must succumb. If not today, then tomorrow or the next day.

And so Priya followed. But he looked back often.

The white man lived in a cabana. Priya had never entered a cabana before. Anything could scare him away. The man knew this. For the moment he did not talk, he just walked up the steps on to the narrow balcony and dropped into the sun-seat. It was cooler here than on the beach. Coconut fronds weaved criss-cross shadows. Priya looked about him timidly. From where he stood he could see into the bedroom. On the bedside table were the promised chocolates, the cigarettes and chewing gum. There was also a bowl of fruit. Priya licked his lips. The man's eyes followed the child's. 'Not yet, not yet,' he said, now confident of conquest. After a while he stood up, looked around the beach furtively and walked into the cabana. Fear welled up in Priya. He half turned to rush down the stairs. Perhaps his mother was already combing the beach for him. The man was knowing and crafty. He held out a chocolate from the bedroom. Priya moved towards it. The man closed the door behind him and dropped the chocolate back into the bowl.

He sat on the bed and drew Priya to him. Priya squirmed but tried to smile and to please, his attention still focussed on the bedside table. He was also excited that he had been employed at last to do the work of the bigger boys. The man was gentle at first. But suddenly he turned Priya around violently, and pushed him down on the bed. He yanked Priya's head back and clamped one hand down over his mouth. All was silent but for rasping gasps. Priya's stiffened stick legs protruded from the bed. As the man impaled him the pain swelled and surged, thrusting relentlessly through his body. And then cessation.

The smell of crushed flowers spilt into the

ensuing stillness. A fly began to buzz around, knocking against panes. Priya lay released at last, his face buried in the sheet. It was the excruciating pain, now, nothing else. He could barely move. The man pulled him to his feet with some impatience. His age demanded that he rest.

'Take the chocolates or the cigarettes,' he said. Priya did not realise that he was dismissed. He swayed and stared. 'Get out,' the man ordered, wanting to be alone. He lay back in the bed and wiped his face as if with sudden distaste for this brown thin child and for the sweat and fish smells that emanated from him. He kicked Priya's shorts from the bed to the floor. Suddenly activated, Priya picked them up and drew them on. He limped up to the table. He picked up a chocolate. His actions were hesitant. He opened the door and crept out. The glare hit his eyes and his world swung back into focus. There was again sound and sense. The crash of waves, the stomach's gnaw, and the ache of Mala.

Simon waited for Priya some distance away from the cabana. Priya stopped short. Tears filled his eyes. He tried to slink away. But Simon held out a few coins. Priya squared his frail shoulders and smiled pathetically.

Aruni asks, 'And what happened to the small baby, Simon? Did he have a name? Did he live?'

'Jamis sold him to a beggar colony, missy,' Simon replies tonelessly. 'We never heard anything more about him. No one wanted to talk about him, or see him. He brought a lot of shame to the family. It was better that way. No, he did not have a right to a name.'

'He was my half-brother. How can it be better that he ended up as a beggar? Can you help me find him?'

'To look for him would be like looking for a grain of sand on the beach.' There is a sense of finality in his tone. He does not tell Aruni how beggar children are crippled by their pimps, their bones broken and twisted out of shape so they will be considered more deserving of charity. He does not tell her the children are pushed around in carts by phoney mothers. He hopes she will let it be. And she does. Her shoulders slump and she lays her head on the arm of his chair.

'What about the twins then?'

'They ran away from the house where they

worked. Asilin and Priya searched everywhere. The convent had no idea. We even inquired at the girls' home up in Magama in case they'd sought refuge there. But we never got any information.'

Simon does not look at Aruni as he speaks. His voice is sunk low, almost to a whisper. It feels stifling hot and he wipes the sweat off his forehead and chest. At last, he bends to her, suspicious of the silence.

Simon takes Aruni to the house where the family had lived. He leaves the door ajar and opens up the windows. Aruni walks here and there – into the centre room and from it to the kitchen, into the backyard, and back in again. In spite of the heat outside, the house is cold and has a musty smell. Simon brings her a cup of tea from the kitchen. She sits on a chair in the centre room seeking footsteps and voices.

In this centre room, Priya had slept his hungers away. In that corner, Mala had lain, wrapped up in the secrets of her body. Here the twins had sat and played, as always lost in their own world, excluding everyone else. And, high up on the wall, was the bright patch where the framed holy picture of the Mother and Child Jesus had hung.

Here where they'd all lived and slept, they had laid out the sealed coffins of Priya's mother and father. Priya leans against the doorway leading to the kitchen.

. . . I am going with your father to Kochichi-kade church to make a vow for Mala, his mother said, pulling out her sari from the trunk that held their more precious belongings. The sari smelt of stale fish and mothballs. After Mala had disappeared that last time, his mother regularly dragged his father to Colombo. She hoped Mala would visit the house if she heard of their father's absence. We'll be back before it gets dark, she said. If it gets a little late, go to Simon's house. It was like any other day.

As usual, though Priya sat at the front doorstep long past lunch time, Mala did not come. At last he served himself some rice and sambol that his mother had left in the chatti-pots for him. As night fell, he walked with Simon to the top of the road. Any moment now his parents would turn the corner, and then he could end his day. They listened to the trains rumbling tiredly in and out of the station in town. And watched them, too, as they passed by, bodies drooping dimly in the squares of windows. Simon flashed his torch now and then on stragglers returning home. They swayed drunkenly and muttered. But Priya's mother and father did not return, and Priya had to sleep in Simon's house. He twitched through the night feeling his mother shaking him awake. In the morning the wireless announced the suicide bombing at Kochichikade.

They identified the bodies by the silver cross still hanging from Asilin's neck, and a piece of sarong sodden with blood. The coffins could not be opened because no one knew how much of the corpses had been recovered, and in what stage of putrefaction they were. Father Lucien and the sisters from the convent brought a wreath of white flowers, said their prayers, and led the funeral procession.

And Priya? Days after consoling neighbours had returned to their own lives, he sat sealed up in the house. Simon sat with him. When Simon asked him to eat he said he was waiting for his mother to return from the market. When Simon asked him to sleep, he said that he would sleep when Mala returned home. All night, the wind rattled the windows, and whistled through the cracks. Priya stared at the red flame sputtering in its bowl before the Mary and Baby Jesus picture in the crevice in the wall . . .

'A few days after the funeral, your father came to see me, missy. They'd heard of the deaths from the convent sisters, and he gave me some money for Priya. But I did not take it. I told him that the government would pay compensation. He did not ask about your mother.'

'I think he came to the beach many times after that,' Aruni says. She surrenders to her own remembering. She knows her father walked with her on this beach. Hanging on to his hand, she prattled about this and that, the shells and small sideways-running crabs, the fat jellyfish shining transparently in the sun. Must she ask so many questions always? But then her father stopped listening. And he stopped walking, at some distance like this, from the village. He looked at the fishing huts a long time. Aruni remembers that he talked to someone. She remembers the low verandah and a wooden bed. But she can't remember who had come out of the house to talk to him. A last bit of memory, though, is etched indelibly. The way her father lifted her and held her tight against his chest, even though she was too big to be carried, with legs dangling down to his knees. And how she rubbed his eyes for him.

The smouldering sun is a smudge in the sky.

She sits very still, looking down, and refuses to

meet Simon's eyes. If only we could heal one another by touch or prayer. There must be a curse buried deep in that family, he thinks. Even those at its edge are not spared.

Aruni's beach cloth billows as the wind rises. The beach is getting ready for a storm. The wind is whipping up the coconut trees. Aruni watches the palms up above, flinging their crests like lunatics. The waves rise high, gather force and assault the beach. Tourists scuttle towards the cabanas and hotels, the local women hurry past with their bags of clothes. Some beach boys seek safety in the watekeiya trees. They creep in between the monstrous roots and seek out a bottle buried in the sand. They pass it around, and the lightning flashes a silver spark on glass. And on predatory eyes, that shine dully.

'Let's go, missy,' Simon says gently, 'it is getting late. Here, help me with my chair. I am tired with all this remembering.'

But it is Priya who comes up to carry away the chair.

'I'll do that,' he says. His voice is curt with warning. As if Aruni had no right to do things for Simon. She backs away uncertainly.

'I'll go now and come back tomorrow,' she says.

As usual, Priya does not acknowledge her farewell.

'All right,' Simon replies, his voice soft in the gathering storm. 'We will be here. We'll still be here.'

She leaves them then, forlorn, and begins to run along the beach back to the hotel.

'Are you frightened? Do you want me to go with you?' Simon shouts after her, but she rushes away. Paul, she thinks hysterically, and the hotel. Even as she runs, the storm breaks. It's nothing like she has known in Melbourne. She presses her ears against the terrifying thunder. The blackened sky shivers, cracks and breaks up into violent streaks of light. 'On stormy nights, Aruni,' her father's voice, half-smothered by the storm, reaches her, 'when it rains cats and dogs, the turtle goes under the water to its other world, so silent, and so calm. And when the rain falls like stones on the sea, the turtle goes even further down to the coral land and sits there singing a turtle song. And all the little fishes settle around her and hide close under her shell . . .'

At last, at last she sights the hotel, and Paul, against the warm globes of garden light. Her body glistens with the winging of her flight. Her wet hair glitters stars in its depths. She runs into the warm dry towel Paul has ready for her. He scolds her, and wraps her in it. He wipes her face and tries to make out if her eyes are red with tears or rain. He draws her to him. She hides her face in his shoulder.

Aruni withdraws into herself. She tells Paul that she has things to do. Books to read, letters to write. She prefers to eat alone at a table, a book open at her side, earphones on, or she orders her food to her room. And he sees her in the morning, walking out of the hotel towards the town instead of down to the beach. When she does not come down to dinner, he knocks at her door late in the night. Perhaps she'd like a brandy with him, or a turn in the garden? Not tonight, she says, she's tired, or she's reading.

She's sitting in the window seat in the semi-darkness, crushed paper collecting in heaps around her. *Dear Dad*, she begins. *With love, Aruni* – she ends. She sucks on her pen, staring for hours at the wonder of moonlight on waves, or the star-spangled sky. In the early hours of the morning she collects all the uncrushed paper in a folder. Sometimes she presses between them a flower she's brought back to the room, or a bookmark she knows her father will like. But she does not post any of it. She sticks up against the wall each postcard he sends her, of those places she loved in Melbourne. But she does not reply. Nor does she tell him much when he telephones her. He wants to come over – he's concerned for her safety. But no, she says, I have to do this alone. She is happy here, in a way. I have made friends. She smiles thinking of Paul, and of Premasiri. Two homes right there, she thinks whimsically. I will write to you, she says, one day, soon. She does not inquire about Neela. Be careful, he pleads, please be careful. She knows. She's protected. She replaces the receiver on his voice.

Paul wonders away, missing her. He calls Melbourne and he and Jo talk for a few minutes about Sue and how she's going in her tennis, her swimming. She's going to be a beach goddess, Jo says. He says that in that case, he'd better get her some bath cloths from the beach. A few for Mum as well. Arty Melbourne is in full swing she says. And Melbourne

Cup's just around the corner. Bet for me, he says. Miss you, Paul, she says. Yep, he replies. She does not offer to come over, and he does not invite her. He replaces the receiver, warmed by her voice so close to his. He lifts it again to tell her something else, but the phone gives back a disconnected tone. Her absence, the missed moment, mist the air.

And then, when he's just getting used to his routine of swimming alone, or reading and walking and eating, Aruni returns. He is happy she is back. And so is she, it seems.

'Tell me, Aruni,' Paul says, having listened to a segment of Aruni's story. 'Do you feel anything for Priya? I mean him being your uncle and that?'

She pulls at her spiky hair. She says she'd come to Sri Lanka yearning to connect with the family she's never known. Paul watches her lazily as moods flit across her face. And her eyes, he thinks, they're Priya's eyes before they died on him. Yet it seems as though there's really no one to connect with, Aruni goes on. But then she says lightly, 'He reminds me of the mariner, Paul. Clinging to the mast of his haunted ship, so wanting to hide – but so exposed.'

'But the end of the poem – the mariner was saved, wasn't he?'

'No, not entirely. He just lived to tell the tale.'

Aruni edges closer to Paul on the stone ledge. Their legs dangle over and their hands lie close together on the rough stone. Suddenly, Aruni tilts her head on to his shoulder. Moved, he lets her be. Poor fish caught in a vast indifferent sea surging and receding with cross currents. She sways a leg and moves it against his. Still in a musing mood, he lets his own respond. She smiles to see their legs touching, like new lovers.

Paul catches the smile. But a thought out of nowhere unnerves him. A chrysalis in a cocoon, he thinks. Insulated, cottoned, inert. But for the passions accumulating within, secretly.

But how foolish his fears! Moonlight filters into the garden as from some purifying blue filter. The very air glistens with it. He puts his arm around her and draws her close. It is cool tonight, and innocent still.

There is a grand weekend buffet at the hotel. The garden is dressed up to meet any tourist's idea of paradise in the tropics. Great golden globes shining dimly here and there on the lawn, the moths and the fireflies flitting around, the coconut palms overhead, the frangipani spreading an insidious perfume all over the garden.

Paul is being disturbed with a longing that has surfaced almost without his awareness. More shocking to him is that he feels no resistance. He longs for a friend in whom he could confide. More and more he seeks Aruni's company.

He lies on a sun-seat at the end of the garden. From the distance, the breeze wafts her perfume to him. He closes his eyes and waits. He suddenly feels her wrist against his face, but it is not perfume that he now inhales. It is the scent of her, warm and heady, unfamiliar and young, and it comes from the beach. He brushes his lips against her wrist. He feels her soft touch, skin on skin. He opens his eyes, and her face is very close to his. Her eyes, level, close up, are like fragile vases he could fill anyway he wanted. Ashamed, he casts the thought aside.

'Gotcha,' she says, rumpling his hair. 'Thought you were dead, Paul. There's a turtle on the beach, want to see?' She pulls at his hand.

They walk towards the small gathering at the hotel's boundary. There are tourists, a waiter or two, a security guard, and a few villagers.

The turtle is forced upside down. It keeps flapping its short stumps against its inner sides. It's one massive turtle. Even the locals haven't seen anything so big for months. Everyone is fascinated by its size, its ugliness. The face peers out of its carapace, obscene and beaky, with large wrinkled jowls. And the eyes – dull dinosaur eyes with ageless lower lids. It struggles to turn right side up, beating its fins frantically. The beach boys hold it down. Premasiri gives them orders and shakes hands and chats with tourists. When he sees Aruni he comes up at once. He shakes hands with Paul, politely requests a cigarette. Paul has none left, and offers him his half-smoked stub. Premasiri takes it with a charming smile that he shares mainly with Aruni and draws on it. Then he teasingly blows a misty tendril in her face. She breathes it in. Her face is blurred and beautiful in the halo of smoke. 'There,' she says, 'we've smoked one cigarette.' He talks exclusively to her. Paul turns back to the turtle show. Aruni asks him to give five hundred rupees to the small boy flitting around like an insect, his palm stretched out. Paul looks at her quizzically – isn't that a lot of money to pay for a glimpse of a fucked-up turtle?

'Premasiri says that if he makes more than five hundred rupees, he will set the turtle free,' she says, her voice cold, defensive. Had she taken a shine to Premasiri then? Paul glances from one to the other.

He does as she asks, but is quite sure they will not free the turtle. They will force it away to another hotel, and then when it is exhausted and starved, they'll dismember it for the meat. It crosses his mind for the first time that Aruni really does belong to these strangers. He is just the tourist with money to spend. He feels shaken, about her, and himself. Perhaps, if he returned in two years, he'd see her right here, dressed in the faded cloth and blouse of a beach woman, trading turtle with the tourists. He could see her inserting her hand into the jagged wound of a slaughtered turtle, scooping out its thickly clotting blood. She weighs the flesh that's cut out – pieces of fin and tail and organs. They say the turtle lives through it all, mourning and writhing in agony, until the carapace is almost empty, until at last, the very heart has been cut out. They know it is alive because it keeps snapping its mouth, and opening and closing its eyelids . . . Paul stares at the tears dripping from the turtle's eyes – it seems aware of its fate.

He needs to return to the hotel. He turns to tell Aruni that he's had enough for one evening. She is gazing wide-eyed at the animal. He is hushed by her expression. It looks more pathetic than the turtle's. He's got used to her orphaned eyes. Now, he is at the edge of something else.

'Let's go, darling,' he whispers to her.

How she caught at the heartstrings at unexpected moments like this. She turns towards him then, and lays her face against his shoulder – a gesture he's getting used to, often meaningless. He puts his arm around her, hoping she hasn't heard the endearment, and its tenderness.

'You called me darling, Paul,' she says blithely, as he leads her back to the buffet. The wetness in her eyes makes them glow like the lamps around them, warm and liquid.

Bugger, thinks Paul. 'Didn't mean anything, possum, thought you were Sue for a bit there.' He makes his voice light, casual.

'Oh.' Aruni wriggles out of his arm, and strides ahead towards the tables laid out under the trees. He hopes he hasn't mucked up the evening.

But he has misgivings as he walks up to her. Who's trying to fool whom here? She is not a kid, had never been a kid. He just tried to force her to be one. It was safer for him.

Dinner is a leisurely affair, with Aruni in a suddenly sparkling mood, guiding Paul into the highly spiced curry. Darling, he'd said, and she'd touched its texture – like velvet. She does not think to question but takes flight in it, excited.

Paul eats like a local, just for the fun of it, using his fingers. She is delighted. They drink a lot of beer to cool it all down. Either a glass of cold water, or beer, that's what goes with rice and curry, she says as though imparting some profound philosophy. She leans towards him, serving him, irresistibly.

It is good to see her unravel, Paul reflects. Savour the birth of a woman.

It's late. The frangipani is unlike anything Paul has seen or smelt back home. The scent is strong and sharp, and spreads with the wind. And you have to pause, pause and let it in. Aruni wears one in her hair. White petalled, opening on a powdery gold heart, it smiles, innocent and seductive. Paul dimly remembers a Maugham story – a Britisher degenerating into a drunk after being seduced by a flower maiden of the tropics. She'd worn a red hibiscus in her hair.

'So?' Aruni says drowsily from the depths of

her armchair. There is music, a woman's voice crooning from afar. He understands nothing of what she sings. Aruni listens, her head to one side. The song's about us, she says, but does not elaborate. Her eyes are as open as they could be, like lagoons.

'So?' He stands up and holds out his hand to her. She stretches and moves into his arms. There is no resistance; she'd go where he led her. Chasing ghosts, Paul bends to her face. He feels her lips, unfamiliar, searching like an infant sucking its first sweet milk. Out of nowhere, a fragment of verse: 'As heaven kisses the sea, softly and quietly as dew kisses, solemnly as the sea kisses the image of the moon'. The poet floats away. Her hands love his skin and wander over it, discovering the pleasures of touch. The sea is all around them, gentle tonight, and silvery blue. It pours into Paul – as through a shell held close to the ear.

Paul shifts slightly. He knows he has nothing to offer her, nothing with which to fill her eyes. She gazes into his face, waiting. Again he remembers that bowl on his windowsill always waiting to be filled by him, or Jo or Sue with whatever of the moment – pins, flowers, chips, chocolates. She smiles, a small sweet smile that extinguishes his reluctance, his hesitation. It beckons him to open up and let her inside. Again he looks away. Still, she holds his hand and looks at him. And curls her fingers around his.

Like a nurse's hand, Aruni thinks dreamily, hanging on to it. A hand that can soothe a child's hot dry forehead like a cloth dipped in eau-de-cologne.

He lies by her, not moving. She sleeps but her hair is awake and catches in his lips every now and then. It grows in the night, secretly, like dolly hair. She giggled when he commented that it was getting longer, no longer sticking up in spikes, thank God. Child: woman. He draws his lips away, so as not to disturb her, and the moment. He had not known of an emptiness within him. But he knows it is filled now, with sadness and joy and aloneness, and that he will be aware of it for the rest of his life.

As if unleashed, Aruni rushes headlong into a festive night on the beach. Most times, Aruni and Paul stood on the periphery watching. Tonight, Aruni joins in the revelries. Boldly, she joins in the baila dance with Premasiri. Paul watches the way her body slants towards his on the drunken beach. Premasiri's eyes, bloodshot, are focused on her. Paul imagines the eyes of a dingo. But she, delighted with her body, tipsy with toddy, follows his steps in some raunchy dance. Swinging, now left, now right, now back. Now she leans towards him, now withdraws, boisterous – all giving, all taking. The young men close around them in a circle. The drums and the clapping charge the air, the lamps swing in the wind, and Paul lies back on the beach exhausted and reeling a little from the toddy. He drains the glass, and spits out the dregs. Premasiri drinks off the bottle, and offers it to Aruni. She drinks and her lips wetly shine. The night ripples in the lamp-light, voluptuous. Paul closes his eyes. As the dance ends, the rhythm rises to a bawdy crescendo – the clapping of metal spoons one against the other becomes louder and louder, the voices and the whistling, raw and raucous. Suddenly she drops on the sand by his side. 'That was wild, man, you should've tried it.' Her skin emanates the sweat and smell of the beach – that strong sticky odour. Paul turns away, repelled. He hears the roar of an airplane in the sky and follows its distant twinkling lights, wishing it was carrying him back to the safety of his home.

Sharing Aruni's bed, Paul spends a restless

night. Perhaps she would change with all this contact with the locals into what her mother had been – a lusty beach woman, ridiculed even by the beach world. This is something that occurs to him more and more. She led him on, and now flirts with the men on the beach, without a care for what he may feel. Did she understand nothing? Paul can't lie in this bed any more with this woman who has already deserted him. But even as he watches her leaden-eyed, she reverts into a child again. He would not have been surprised had she started sucking her thumb in her sleep. He edges out of bed, untangling himself from her arms. She turns and sighs, wraps herself in the covering sheet, and sleeps.

Paul sits by the window. There is nothing outside that he can relate to. Sand and sea and sky have merged into one endless void. He checks the clock. It would still be late evening for Jo and Sue back in Melbourne. Were they missing him? It's Saturday. Sue is probably out partying. And Jo? Curled up in the couch in the family room. Was she thinking about him? Missing the footy, the late night show. He'd go to reception to try that overseas line, blocked now for days. But as he moves towards the door, Aruni opens her eyes. He lies down again beside her.

He untangles the sheet and spreads it over them both. She places his hand under her cheek, smiles and is still. Paul does not want to go out into the darkness any more.

All night the waves smash the silence. Paul yearns for respite. And gradually the sky clears, the windows frame squares of pale moonlight, and the glittering miracle of the star-dusted sky. Sue named stars after her best friends, and they changed from year to year until he never knew which was which. He'd shown her the Southern Cross, kneeling close beside her, his eyes level with hers. In another life, light years away. He thinks he spies a shooting star but can't be sure. 'Make a wish, Paul.' 'What d'ya wish, Dad?' Beloved voices, closer than they'd ever been. He shuts his eyes.

As dawn breaks, he is at the window again. The day dawns in luxurious abandonment, without the agony of a human birth. The sun is born in the swirl of a wave. It curls out of the silvery womb. Paul feels privy to the most private secrets of this land, to the joy of all her giving.

Aruni comes up behind him. 'What are you doing up so early, Paul?' she asks. Then, seeing his pensive face, 'Were you thinking about your family?'

Paul takes her hand. 'No,' he says. 'Just conse-crating my day to you, petal.'

But as he pushes back the heavy curtains, the light, flooding into the room, has the sheen of his daughter's hair.

This morning, instead of making her usual pilgrimage up the beach to Simon and Priya, Aruni sits in the shade of the hotel garden and reads *What the Buddha Said*. Happy with this bit of tranquility, Paul lies beside her on a sun-seat. He takes her book, and reads the opened page: '*There are three spheres of consciousness: the sensuous sphere, the form sphere, and the formless sphere. Desire plays a major part in the movement from one sphere to another. The form-less sphere is the highest consciousness. It liberates you even from desire.*'

He tries half-heartedly to digest this wisdom. The catchword for him, just at the moment, he thinks, is desire – in all its forms. He wonders when he will be liberated into the next sphere. What comes before, what after. He touches Aruni's leg or arm lying by his side, for no reason at all. And occasionally she glances

137

up and smiles. He rustles the newspaper and hides behind it. The government still negotiating peace, he reads on every page – this country, so small but so territorial. Where were they all going, carrying their bits of land? From nowhere to nowhere, like a trail of ants. On the next page, a triumphant photograph captures all that's precious between a mother and child. He reads the effusive caption – a test-tube baby has lived out her first three months and is thriving. He wonders whether, eighteen years from now, the test-tube girl will rush around the world, tearing people's lives apart while she searches for the father she's never seen.

Aruni turns to him. And she lets Paul into her other life, from which she insists she's broken free. There is a lot she doesn't know about Neela and Mohan and Mala, she says, a lot that she's tried to imagine for as long as she can remember.

'There was always music, Paul,' she says, 'when I was a little girl.'

p a r t t w o

There was music. It floated around Neela and caressed her like baby breath. It was Mohan's song, and she listened as she drifted somewhere between sleep and waking. The melody felt mulled. There was a fragrance, a muted hue to Mohan's voice when he sang in the still hot nights. Then Aruni's childish treble joined in, and Neela awakened fully to the two voices downstairs, so inextricably blended. Again she surrendered to the memory that was Nirmala.

Neela sat by the window flicking through a magazine. She was expecting the new servant girl this morning from the convent. She looked impatiently towards the gates and glanced at her watch yet again. She began to walk around the hall, turning a cushion here, moving a vase there, and paused at the grand piano. She opened the lid, and glided her fingers silently across the keys. She looked up instinctively at the photograph of her little girl, now dead. And she died one more death.

The doorbell rang once, and then again. Neela awakened to it gradually. She glanced at the time, wondering, as she opened the door, why servants could never be punctual. The first impression was not favourable. The girl looked sullen and angry and stood in the driveway staring at her feet. Simon was at the door.

'This is the girl, madam, from the convent,' he said.

'Yes, yes, come round the back,' Neela answered, withdrawing into the house and closing the door. She received Simon and Mala at the back door, and invited them into the kitchen area. An old servant woman hovered in the background.

Neela tried to size up the girl. But Mala was heavily silent, ungiving.

'Do you want to stay and work in this house?'

Neela asked finally, irritated.

'Yes,' Mala muttered, but with no enthusiasm.

'What is your name?'

'Nirmala . . . But they call me Mala.'

'Good. And where is your mother?' Neela was trying to decide whether she wanted the girl in her house. What would Mohan say? They had tried out a church girl of about the same age as this before, and she'd run away only weeks later, taking Neela's cultured pearl necklace with her. So much for good Catholic orphans, Mohan had laughed. But after her initial anger, Neela had not really blamed the girl. Perhaps they'd all go thieving if they had nothing to call their own and had to live with people who had too much. Serves me right for being so careless, she said to Mohan. It had been one of those precious moments of connection between herself and Mohan, which could never be lost, whatever happened. He'd reached for her hand, and looked at her with respect and affection.

But after that, they'd steered clear of church girls. And yet, when Sister Mercy related Mala's story to her, Neela had been moved. The girl had never known any better, and had got into trouble. She was a brave girl. And the church had been helping the family for a long time. The mother was hardworking and did all she could to make ends meet. But when the girl got into trouble her father, a no-good drunk, had driven her out of the house. Now, the mother was forced to tend the unfortunate baby. Sister Mercy felt that Mala could make a new life with a good family, like Neela and Mohan's. She deserved a second chance.

'Her mother has three other children and the baby to look after, hamu. Please help the family. This is a good Catholic girl,' Simon persuaded in a low voice.

It was a wrench to hand Mala over to strangers. He'd found her lying half dead on his verandah. When he bent over her, she wound her arms around him, whimpering through cracked lips. Deserting the baby at her mother's doorstep, she'd sought shelter on his. I thought you'd run away to the convent after the big fight in the house, he murmured to her. Yes, and they sent me away to have the baby in a girls' home. But I couldn't stay there any more. Had to come home, aiye, come home, she sobbed. Come home.

'Let her stay then. Stay and drink a cup of tea before you go,' Neela said, making an impulsive decision. 'Simon, I have some old clothes that you can take back to the convent. Mala, I will find a cloth that you can wrap over that skirt for the moment. There's the servant's bathroom, out there in the garden. Go and take a bath before you wear it. Menika, get the tea things ready.' And they submitted to her self-assured efficiency.

'I will come and see you often, you will be happy here,' Simon said to Mala, respectfully bowing to Neela.

'Yes, then I can send some money home to her family. Come at the end of the month, Simon,' Neela said.

Menika woke Mala early the next morning. She must carry the tea tray to the bedroom, Menika told her. As she climbed the staircase, step by careful step, Mala passed a series of framed photographs hanging on the wall. They were of the dead child. Mala did not pause. She was afraid the tea would cool. She stood at the door and called, 'Hamu, here's the tea,' and entered the room hesitantly. From the doorway, she saw the ornate double bed and the master, sitting up in it, his face buried in a newspaper. Mala was very aware of the white sheets and pillows, so clean and fresh. Neela smiled and asked her to bring the tray to her side of the bed. Mala put it on the side table, and began to edge out of the room.

'Tell Menika to lay the table for breakfast,' Neela said in a friendly tone.

'Yes, hamu.' Mala caught her smile and shyly held it. It engaged her heart. No one smiled much in her own house.

As she walked out of the room, she heard the lady ask in English, 'Mohan, do you think she'll be all right?'

She paused to hear him say, 'Who's to know, Neela? Try her out and see, if that's what you want.' And then the rustle of paper.

Mala went down the stairs slowly, stopping to look at the row of photographs. She knew the child's name had been Kumari. There were many pictures of her as an infant, in lace dress, booties and tiny hat, in Neela's arms, Mohan's and Menika's. Others showed her at each birthday, growing bit by bit. In frilly frocks and ribbons she stood at a small table smiling widely, just before cutting the cake. And to what trouble had they gone with the cake decorations. How happily everyone beamed into the camera. Mala stood back against the banister, drinking in all this joy. She drew closer, and counted seven candles on the last cake. And then no more cakes, and no more photographs. The family had stopped smiling. She drew aside the curtains on the landing, so bright sun spots fell on the pictures, and went down the rest of the stairs, crossed the spacious hall and dining room into the kitchen area.

It seemed to her a very long walk. Ten steps, she thought, from front to back door of her own house. Priya would be sniffling around hungrily at this time of morning, rubbing the sleep from his eyes, and their mother would be yelling at him to pick up the half-caste and give it some tea-water while, in the darkness of the kitchen, she settled the jadi fish in the chatti-pot. Or, would she be sitting on the back doorstep, pulling out the entrails of a medium-sized fish, making space in it for salt crystals? The smells would invade the house and draw saliva to their lips. Later, she and Mala would go down to the lagoon to thump the coconut husks for rope twisting. Or maybe her mother would push her to complete weaving the coconut frond to block the roof that had sprung a leak. Or else, with the next downpour, through the day and night, the rain would drop tok tok tok into the bucket below.

'So many pictures of the baba,' she said to Menika. 'You'd think she was still alive.'

'She's alive in all of us, right here,' said Menika, her hand pressed to her breast.

Mohan and Neela sat down to their breakfast with Menika hovering around. Mala stood just behind the kitchen door, not knowing what was expected of her. After a little while, she looked into the dining room. She absorbed a cameo of domesticity. Neela was just serving her husband a few more string-hoppers in spite of his gentle protest. They sat close together, he at the head of the table, and she at his side. They did not talk much. Mala missed all the noise of her own home; the squabbles, the greed, the running around and getting entangled in one another's bodies. In this vast mansion, it was all so deadly silent. She felt sorry for Neela, eating delicately at the richly carved table, as if it were a task that had to be performed. Did she even taste the two hours of labour that Menika had put into this string-hopper breakfast?

When the master asked for a glass of water, Menika indicated to Mala with her eyes.

Mala jumped into action. She filled a glass with iced water, wiped it with the cloth, and placed it on a white saucer. With both hands, she took the water to him. He looked up at her briefly, acknowledging it. She cast down her eyes, but not before she'd seen into the depths of his. Fleetingly, she recalled Simon. As she stood behind the door, once again, she kept looking at him, as though drinking cool fresh water out of a fountain.

That night Mala cried herself to sleep in the back room. The grand old house was empty but for the lady, the master and the old woman, and the pictures of the dead little girl. It seemed to Mala that the dead child was the only one alive in the house. The furniture looked as if it had not been moved for generations. Mala was overcome by the grandeur of it all. She was sleeping for the first time in her life on a bed, hard and narrow, and though she felt the comfort of a real mattress, she missed the freedom of her mat. She missed Priya and her mother and sisters, and all the sleep sounds they made. She wondered whether Priya would look after the half-caste as he had said he would. He was still a little boy himself, and given to long spells of staring inwards. She turned sleeplessly on her bed. There, against the opposite wall, the old servant lay.

'You will have to get used to the work quickly.

I must soon go back to my village to tend my sick daughter,' she said to Mala. 'You know, when I first went to the old walauwa to look after our hamu, she was just a girl. And then, when she got married, she brought me here. I looked after Kumari baba till she died two years ago. Oh, the little one. How I long to see her – a bundle of mischief she was. She'd be sitting on my bed now, if she were here, demanding a story, and not caring how tired I was after all the cooking and the cleaning.' The old voice sighed. 'I feel she's sitting here, like she used to, jabbering away about this and that.'

Mala dreamt of the beach that night. She floated as to a lullaby as her father rowed a boat one tranquil night at sea. She leaned out of its edge and watched the sea life sparkling past in the light of the full moon. At last, they drew in on Lihiniya Island. She rode her father's shoulders as he followed the laboured curved tracks of a turtle. She carried a basket that smelt of egg yolk and unhatched baby turtles. They moved in quietly. The turtle was laying white ping-pong eggs in its sandy nest. Mala and her father sat by for hours, silently, waiting for the turtle to move away. Then they picked up the eggs and laid them in the basket. The dream switched. They'd got to the beach too late. The eggs had already hatched under the sand and they could only look on as dozens of tiny turtles crawled out and headed clumsily towards the moonlit sea. They watched the lonely eagles swoop down from the crags. They searched for the mother turtle that always returned to the nest at the time of hatching. But they could not find her. Mala woke up sobbing.

'It's a good life, Mala, child,' Menika said the next day. 'The lady and master are kind people and you will be very happy here. Here, eat and get some flesh on those bones.' And she handed Mala her plate of rice and curry.

Mala's eyes grew round and foolish as she gaped at the food. Would she ever get used to being served so many curries heaped on so much rice? Even the convent sisters ate frugally, a bit of rice, a meat or fish curry, one watery vegetable and a mallum. She took the plate shyly and retired to a corner. As she stood swallowing the food, Menika drew up the coconut scraper for her. Mala sat on its narrow plank, dipped her fingers in the rice, and pushed large portions into her mouth. Pulling out a fish bone from the rice, she looked up and smiled a wide, charming smile.

'Eat slowly, Mala child, there are no demons

lurking outside the window to carry away your plate,' Menika chuckled.

Mala slowed down to chew the rice – she felt at home with Menika. She was like any old crone in the village. She was about to tell her so, when Neela walked in, and she and Menika stood up respectfully.

The nights and days spread into each other. Mala got used to the house and the people who lived such different lives from hers. The days were easier than the nights. She was too busy to think about anything. There was a lot to do, learning the housework from Menika. There was Banda the gardener to chat with over a sip of tea. But in the nights, her breasts were so swollen and heavy. In the loneliest moments, Mala squeezed them, biting the pillow to stifle the pain, as if to force out the hardened milk.

One night, drawing the sheet around her, she got out of bed, and slid out of the back door. She stood in the garden under the rambutan tree that Aruni would come to love. She picked a ripe rambutan off the ground, bit open its skin and ate the soft white flesh. Relishing its sweetness, she turned in a slow pirouette. Banda had trimmed the back garden only this morning and it swept away from the house and even further, beyond the paved pathway towards the vegetable plots. There was a slither of moon, and as she gazed at it, Mala remembered how, on such nights, she would pull Priya blindfolded out on to the beach, and turn his face towards the moon before removing the blindfold. He would then look straight up at the moon, and turn to beam with her. Because they said that if you looked at the crescent moon and caught someone's beautiful smile, good fortune would shower on you.

'Mala akke, you have such a beautiful smile,' Priya breathed, overcome with affection for her, and thrilled to be treated to her abundance. She remembered also how often she'd rush him out and hold up a broom to his face, so that when he opened his eyes, the first thing he saw was its dirt-sweeping end. And how she laughed to see his tears. How easily Priya cried, and how easily he made her feel guilty. She sighed now, remembering his neediness, and the two useless sisters who had each other and needed no one else. She hoped the half-caste would die. Fatherless, motherless, and foodless, Priya would chant, rocking it to sleep on his stretched-out legs. She shrugged away the memory, and walked towards the vegetable plot. At the very end of the garden grew the massive jak tree that had gone barren since Kumari's death. The road light fell on this side of the garden, and the silhouetted branches drooped tiredly. Mala sat on the rock beneath it and leaning against its trunk, began to sing.

> *Sleep, my baby, sleep*
> *Listen to the wind in the sail*
> *Your father is away at sea*
> *The moon runs on the water.*

The lonely night wept to the gurgle of infants and the fragrance of suckling lips.

Mala massaged Neela's feet or rubbed oil into her hair in the long hot afternoons. Neela asked her idly about her life back home and about the baby she'd left behind. Once she felt released from her awe of the lady, Mala talked a lot. She told Neela of her brother Priya and how she'd brought him up, of their mother and father and the twins, the difficulties of their lives

– the poverty, the empty stomachs and their faith in the Holy Mary.

'I have been there only once before,' she said, after a visit to Colombo with Neela. 'And that was when I was little. We went to St Anthony's Kochchichikade, my mother, my father, Priya and I. It was to protect our father from the ganja, my mother said. A lot of the beach boys were addicted, and they peddled it to anyone who'd give them money. We all knew that our father peddled occasionally and that our mother, if she got hold of it, used the money he made to buy things for the house. But she wanted him to stay clean. My mother is always on the lookout – but I know he's not on drugs, hamu – because otherwise he'd turn thin and drippy, and limp about the beach.

'But that day we went to Colombo is like a dream to me. Everything was so crowded, and everyone rushed everywhere. Cars and lorries and bicycles, one on top of the other. My head spun. I got so frightened when I lost my father's hand. I started screaming but no one cared. I was thronged in. There was the sweat-smell but it wasn't the sweat-smell of my father. But then, I was suddenly lifted into the skies by a pair of hands, and they were his! I laughed and cried and laughed. Kelle, kelle, he crooned to me, lifting me astride on his shoulder, did you think I'd let you go? I was still sobbing when we entered the church.

'The church was gloomy and huge, and smelt of burning candles and garlands of jasmine flowers. My mother knelt down and prayed for a long time. She made me tell the Holy Marys after she recited the Hail Marys. But sometimes I forgot my prayer – her face looked so sad, hamu – I felt like crying. After each decade she stopped and offered up the next one for our father. He never prayed. He came up to give us the garlands he had bought. He did not know of course that we were praying for him! I held them and they smelt so fine, like how you smell in dreams. I stuck my face in them. I prayed to St Anthony to plant a jasmine tree in our back garden. But of course I knew this would not happen. How could jasmine grow on the beach? And where was the room for it in our backyard? No, miracles happen only in church books, hamu.

'After that, my mother went to garland the baby St Anthony statue and touch his feet three times. She lifted me and Priya and made us do the same. She put two rupees in the till. Tell St Anthony that we will come back next year to fulfill the vow and put in another two rupees, she said. I prayed and prayed, even though I thought that St Anthony looked very grand in his silk cloak and gold chains, and didn't need our two rupees. If he gave us one of his chains, my father would not have to sell drugs. Priya could go to school and study and be a car driver like Simon. But then I got frightened and asked St Anthony to cancel out the last thoughts or pretend he hadn't heard them. I looked sideways at my father. He did not kneel. He just stood in the shadows and stared at all the people. My mother said he turned into an idiot when the sea was out of his sight.

'Outside the church, he bought me some glass bangles. My mother complained that we needed the money for more important things like tea leaves and juggery. But my father ignored her. Priya wanted an ice-cream, but by then my father had spent all his money. I gave him a bangle to keep him from sniffling. If there is one thing Priya can do, my mother always says, it is sniffle. If the school gave a prize for sniffling, he'd get it every year, she says.

'We made our way through the heap of beggars. They crowded round the big rich cars and left us alone. Rich ladies wearing gold bangles put down the shutters and distributed packets of rice. I saw a beggar who did not get a packet kick the car as it drove off. Everyone glared at everyone else, like prize-fighting cocks ready to kill for a rupee's bet. Even the birds on the wires high up in the sky were shrieking furiously. There were burnt bats hanging from the wires. They stared down with their dead eyes. I only wanted to get away to the beach. Where we belong.'

Mala did not tell Neela about how she had gone with the white men. She liked the lady and master to think that she was a good Catholic girl who had fallen into trouble because of her circumstances. She talked of Simon occasionally in a voice that turned slow and hesitant. So much so, that Neela looked into Mala's face questioningly.

'When you are a little older, Mala, you should go back to the village and marry Simon. He's a kind man, and he'll look after your baby, I'm sure. We have known him for a long time now, through the sisters.'

'No, hamu,' Mala said looking into the distance, 'he wouldn't marry anyone like me. He's . . . he's . . .'

But she would say nothing negative about him. Quickly, she switched back to her baby. Neela sighed when Mala talked of it. Sometimes, there was a playfulness about the way she chattered, as if the baby were no more than a doll. Moved, Neela brought her a small doll one day, telling her, 'There, I know you are too old to play with dolls, Mala, but you can pretend this is your baby.'

Mala took it gratefully enough, but muttered as Neela walked away. 'Aney hamu, if you knew my baby, you'd bring me a rag doll. This one is too beautiful and perfect. Maybe this is your own pretty little Kumari baba.'

Neela stopped in her tracks and turned sharply. Mala cowered. Seeing her face screw up with fear and regret, Neela took a step forward and touched her shoulder. With uncertain fingertips, she wiped the tears collecting on Mala's lashes.

'Maybe that's why I brought the doll for you. Cuddle it anyway, Mala, and imagine then, that it is my Kumari. And sing your songs to her, so I will hear them too.'

Mala cradled the doll or sang it to sleep under the jak tree only when she thought no one was around to see her. But once, when she looked up, Mohan was there at the window, staring down at her with an expression she could not read. Was he thinking of the dead child? Guiltily, Mala stopped singing. But Mohan spread his hands in a graceful outward sweep and she began to sing again. It was not a lullaby any more, but a soulful melody. In the distant hills, a lonely lover awaits a forest girl. And she, seduced by the haunting memory of their love, leaves her work half-done and runs to him. She melts into his arms like a song flowing in the wind.

As Mala sang, the night shimmered into a cataract of music, as if a sitar played in the background, drawing out the pleasure of the lovers. When she looked up again, Mohan was still there, by the window. She felt the hunger in him for more. And at last, the pain in her breasts began to dry up.

That evening, walking about the vegetable plot, Mohan whistled in small sharp spurts the song she'd been singing. It was all Mala could do not to walk behind him, leading him further into it, into the bits of melody that he left out.

Later, much later in the night, they turned in their beds as Mohan began to play the piano, and sing. Mala lay awake roused to emotions she had never felt before – and close to a mute understanding of Mohan and Neela's grief, their lonely anguish for the dead child, and their isolation from each other.

Mohan's song was a lullaby played to a dead child, and with each note the air trembled into light. She thought of her own baby, gasping for life on the mat, its matchstick arms and legs sticking out like fins. She wondered how it still lived when the beautiful child of this house, surrounded by every luxury, had died. She fell asleep to Mohan's song.

Simon visited Mala in the Corner House one Sunday morning. She seemed happy enough. She showed him the doll and talked and laughed easily. Simon told Mala of all the trouble in the house, and how the baby seemed not to know anyone at all, even though it was now over three months. Mala smiled a bitter, older woman's smile, and said she did not care.

Simon gave her other bits of news. 'Your father is drunk from morning till night. And otherwise, he's betting on horses. He gambles away all the money. Never wins a cent.'

'With my money,' Mala said harshly. She felt Simon's eyes on her with that expression she knew so well – the distanced affection of the statues in the chapel. She asked him about Priya. He told her Priya was fine, but missed her. He had wanted to visit her, Simon said, but their mother had stopped him, afraid that the lady would not welcome so many visitors for Mala. She brooded on this a while.

'Be careful he doesn't get caught in the suddha's net,' she said.

Simon sat pensive. From where he sat, he could see into the spacious hall and dining room. He imagined Mala dusting the furniture and sweeping the floors every morning and evening. How she would stare out of the window at the sunset she could only just see over the high roofs. Did she remember those other sunrises and sunsets, and long to be home, where the fishing boats glimmered in the blackness before dawn, and the waves danced to the rhythm of the night goddess? 'I want to be a lady like Neela hamu,' he heard her say. She had wrapped around her waist the new cloth he'd brought her and swayed her body to a slow, secret rhythm.

It was a poya night but the full moon was lost behind thick cloud and so the world was dimly lit. As usual, Mohan had driven Neela to the temple for the all-night pirith. Now that Menika had gone back to her village for a few months, it was left to Mala to get Mohan's dinner ready for when he returned. Mala relished the evening; she felt she was the mistress of the house. She walked around giving imaginary orders to the absent Menika. She paused often, as Neela did, by the photographs of the child. She felt herself caught in Neela's tragic loss. She sighed and stepped away to the grand piano, and lifted the lid. She sat on the stool, and plucked a note or two. Her eyes fell on the photograph on the piano. She touched it with Neela's involved, possessive fingers. She kissed the photograph and wiped her eyes. She stood up and walked around the house. She began to think of the beach, and of Simon and Priya. She felt a kind of jealousy that she was outside it all.

'Once a beach girl, always a beach girl,' the convent sisters had comforted her, when they sent her to this house. 'You'll be back, Mala, because that's what you are, a beach girl.' Mala had smiled a tearful smile. And that's what Menika had often said to her: 'You beach girls always smell of fish. Go take a bath and soap it out.' But Mala knew that Mohan hamu did not think so. She knew he did not mind it when she served him, as she would tonight, standing by his side, or just behind him, anticipating all his needs with an ever greater alertness than Neela. She made herself smell specially nice for the occasion. She felt honoured.

She took her bath, spread her hair down on her back, and tripped up the stairs to the big bedroom. She entered it stealthily, knowing that she was invading a privacy that was not hers. She drew up to the mirror. Timidly, she sat on the stool before it. She saw herself aglow. She powdered her face and neck as she'd seen Neela do. She drew the comb through her hair and smoothed the last wetness from the long strands. She stared at her reflection, seeing how the lashes that framed her eyes were thick and entangled, and how auburn sparkles highlighted the black depths of her hair. She leaned backwards into invisible arms. The mirror filled her dreams, and her robust beauty.

Vaguely, she sensed she'd been in this room before. Maybe, as Neela hamu said, she had been born into this house in an earlier birth, as Neela hamu's younger sister. Or, Mala thought to herself, she might have been Mohan hamu's first wife in a previous birth. Who'd know? There was a higher plan that only God knew, her mother would say.

She walked to the window. She could see herself now as Mohan often saw her, sitting under the jak tree singing her songs. The tree was bearing fruit at last. It had lain barren for so long, and was now bearing a full harvest that never seemed to cease. Large green fruits hung from its trunk. Some of the older fruits, too high for plucking in the first round, had ripened on the tree, and a few were burst open with the luscious golden madulu. When relatives came home, Neela would take them to the jak tree and tell them how Mala's singing had made it fertile again. And when Mohan first heard this, he said something in English that Mala did not understand. And Neela hamu had laughed, and the laugh had held the sound of the silver bells in the hushed chapel back in the village. Mala had watched the way Mohan closed up his newspaper and leaned towards Neela with the softest look in his eyes. And she had closed her own eyes, and savoured his caress on Neela's neck . . .

The door of the almirah was half open. Mala opened it fully. Mohan's shirts, neatly ironed by her, lay folded in a pile. She recognised each one – the smart black and white striped shirt, the deep blue that reminded her of the midnight sky. She touched it now, as it lay right on top of the pile. She smelt his after-shave on it and looking around furtively, pressed her face in it. Then she sped away again, round the room, swaying and humming to herself.

She listened for his car. She'd go down to heat the curries in a moment. She sat down on the big bed, timidly. She'd never done this before, not even when she was alone in the house. But tonight, she felt drawn to it. She smoothed down the sheet where it seemed slightly rumpled as if someone had been sitting on it a moment before. She glanced at the photograph on the bedside table, of Mohan, Neela and little Kumari.

Mohan was late. Mala was beginning to feel sleepy now. She lay back on the big bed, staring at the shadow patterns on the wall. Strange feelings crept over her. She turned sideways and, stretching, kissed the photograph. Her eyes closed. She spread her lips down Mohan's neck and kissed its hollow. Mala knew how Neela must feel when Mohan touched her. She drew her hand down her body, imagining it was Mohan's. And quickly stopped herself. It was as if she suddenly heard her mother's shrill voice. But then, as she lay there, she remembered the hotel rooms back in the village, and the white men who had guided her to taste the secret pleasures of her body. And she moaned, raising her face to be kissed, holding out her breasts to be touched. She pressed her legs together, and then drew them slowly apart. She relished the softness of the mattress and the fragrance of sheets newly washed and ironed.

Mala did not hear Mohan come home. She did not hear him call her name or walk up the stairs. When he stepped into the bedroom, she lay fast asleep, her lips slightly parted. It seemed she smiled with him. A whiff of Neela's perfume hung about the room.

Mohan sat on the bed. He dropped his car keys on the side table and straightened the photograph. Then he turned to Mala. He recognised her blouse. It was one of Neela's cast-offs. Mala breathed deeply in her sleep and he saw the rise and fall of her cupped breasts beneath the thin cotton. Almost without his will, his hand moved to touch her exposed midriff. She stirred but did not awaken. She moaned his name and mumbled about heating the curries. He hush-hushed her, his fingers on her lips. She moved lazily as he bent over her; she surrendered as if to a dream reaching fruition.

The tea slopped on the saucer as Mala carried the tray upstairs. She was nervous. As she entered the room, she saw Mohan alone on the big bed, and heard Neela in the shower. Mohan was not reading the paper this morning. He was staring at the wall opposite. Mala placed the tray on Neela's bedside table. Without looking at her, Mohan reached for the cup and drew away his arm.

Mala turned and closed Neela's cup with the saucer. She waited for a sign. But still he would not look at her. She came up to his side. There was an unreality about it, and she acted as if she were in a film – in the exchange with her lover of an intimate secret. She could see the flower garden and blue skies, birds and butterflies making love, and herself dressed in gauzy golden veils, dancing with him in the sunshine.

But of course, he responded differently. He neither looked at her, nor took her hand in his with surging love. Instead he busied himself with the cup of tea and kept glancing towards the bathroom door. Mala stepped back into the reality of rich white sheets to which she had no claim.

When she realised she was pregnant for the second time, early one sweaty morning, Mala cringed, knees drawn up, arms crushing her head. She bore down with all her strength, trying to expel the thing growing inside her. Nausea rose up in waves and she remembered the first time. She climbed out of bed and ran outside, to the far end of the garden. There, leaning her hands against the jak tree, she began to retch. When at last she straightened, she turned around and gazed up at the windows of Mohan and Neela's bedroom, but there was no one looking out. She slid down to a crouch, her back to the tree. Above, the crows cawed raucously, tearing out the entrails of a ripe jak fruit. Bits of the pulpy madulu fell around her. She stared at them, as in a nightmare. Their overripe smell hung heavily, everywhere. She bore down again and again, spewing bile.

She wiped her lips with the end of her skirt and looked up into Neela's alarmed face. Neela stepped closer and tried to steady her. But Mala fell down on her knees and clasped Neela's feet in supplication.

'Aney hamu,' she cried, her forehead pressed against Neela's feet, 'I am lost again.' Neela placed her hands on Mala's shoulders to raise her to her feet. Their eyes met and held; their suffering souls touched.

They were caught in the cycle of births and deaths – and they were one.

Neela led Mala into the kitchen and prepared her a glass of hot black coffee. As Mala sipped it, Neela wanted to know who'd made her pregnant. Mala stared out of the door in terrified silence. Neela's kindness. Neela's affection. Her simple trust. Mala could not breathe. She tried to concoct a lie, but failed. She jumped up, knocking over her glass. It shattered with a loud crack. The coffee flowed out. She stood for a minute staring down at the mess, and then suddenly turned and ran out of the house. By the time Neela came to the front door, Mala was nowhere to be seen. Neela stood a long time at the gate.

Later she confided in Mohan, trying to rationalise. Perhaps Banda had got her pregnant, she said. She'd often seen Mala and Banda talking under the rambutan tree, when Banda took a rest from mowing or sweeping. Even Menika had hinted at their growing friendship before she went away. Did Mohan think they could be married? Banda must not be allowed to get away with this. He must be made responsible. What did Mohan think? All this must have happened because Menika went away, leaving

the young girl to her own devices, Neela said regret-
fully, trying to pin the blame on someone.

Then she said, these fishing people, they are all
the same, what can you expect from them?

Send the family some money and forget about
it, Mohan heard himself say. His voice sounded normal even to himself. It was he, he thought, gripped
with shame, not Mala, who should fall at Neela's feet
and beg her forgiveness.

Neela listened to him, as always. She served
more rice and curry on his plate. She knew he'd miss
the girl too. But Mohan pushed the plate away as if
he'd seen a long black hair curling in the rice. Neela
said she'd write to Menika and get her back to man-
age the big house. She sighed, thinking of all the work
she'd have to do until then.

Priya dreamt that Mala was dead. No, he cried out,
sitting up in a gasp, she was alive. She was alive – the
wind carried his voice back to him. She was alive. His
dreams swelled in waves and flung her body to him
and then, as he wrapped around her, sucked it back.

'I have a note,' Aruni says to Simon, making sure with a backward glance that Priya is listening. She draws the note from an envelope, hesitantly. She's waited and waited for the right moment. She offers it to Simon, and watches him open out the square of paper. It is yellow at the edges, and crumpled with being touched and retouched. She hopes it will open windows and doors.

'*Neela hamu,*' it began in unformed Sinhalese. The writing was not in a line but ran all over the page. '*Neela hamu,*' it read, the page stabbed here and there when the pencil jabbed through. '*I am leaving my daughter here. Please look after her. Please think of her as your own daughter Kumari who has been reborn. She is Mohan hamu's daughter too.'*

Simon reads aloud but makes no comment. He holds out the note to Priya who stands behind him. But Priya remains still, as if unconscious. The note flutters down. Aruni moves in a rush to grab it before it flies off in the wind. But Priya bends and picks it up. As he stands, Aruni looks into his eyes. They share a moment of his imprisoned past. She cleaves to it. But he escapes. He loses himself in the letter. She yearns and yearns to know the story in him, his story about her mother, and about herself.

'Can you talk to me about it, about this time?'

'No,' Priya says, and limps away towards the giant waves that loom and crash, loom and crash. Suddenly, he dips in. Aruni knows he will not be back on the beach for hours. Nonplussed, she turns away, and returns to the hotel.

It is about that time of night when you realise that you are past sleeping. Paul scribbles at the table. Often his eyes move to Aruni, and the way she slept curled into herself on his bed. At last, he stands up to draw the heavy curtains. He opens the window, and leans out into the darkness, regarding the moonlight on the tattered beach, lighting up the refuse of yet another storm – the coconut leaves and seaweed strewn over the beach, sodden paper bags limp and half-buried in the sand. He smells the salt wind, hot and sticky. He sees shadows moving out of shadows, the hotel security guards gathering to share a glass of warming arak, a beach boy or two glancing surreptitiously at the hotel windows for a lonely tourist. He knows that as soon as it is light, the women will come to drag away the coconut palms that the wind had brought down. He turns back towards Aruni. She sleeps like Sue does. He remembers walking into Sue's room, last thing at night, having snapped shut the lap-top in his study, to draw the quilt up around her neck and switch off her bedside lamp. And he remembers how, before he even reached the door, she'd have thrown the quilt off again.

He feels alienated from this strange girl, as from the night about which he knows so little. He moves to cover her up with the thin sheet. She murmurs, something about St Kilda, her words a-jumble. She'd returned to Melbourne in her dream. He feels a connection, at last, with what is and what was. Her palm lies open at her cheek. He puts his finger in it and like an infant she closes her fist around it. He smiles, and bends to switch off the light. He moves soundlessly out of his room, and into hers.

Priya turned again on the mat, twisting himself into a tangle of bones. He turned yet again, then lifted himself up on his elbow. Mala's half-caste lay just a little distance away. He knew it was hungry – but it was always hungry. He could hear it suck on air as it lay naked on its threadbare cloth. He stretched an arm and tapped the fragile rib cage, until he felt it lulled, the limbs slowly relaxing, the sucking fading into fitful sleep. Leaning further, he felt for the tiny fingers that would grasp his if they could.

He knew it was very late. It was that time of night when even the sound of the sea was subdued by the blanketing darkness. He peered around the room. The flame flickered in the red glass bowl before Mother Mary and Baby Jesus. Shadows played on the picture, and small points of lights sparkled in the eyes of Baby Jesus. Priya's thoughts wandered away to a dream of Mala's baby being transformed into the chubby little Jesus smiling into Mary's face. And Mary – or Mala, if only it could be Mala – gazing down at him in the gloom. If only. He curled up on the cold mat, and seemed to hear her mutter in her sleep and cuddle him anyway. But there was no Mala. It must be five months now since they'd heard she'd run away from the Corner House. They'd searched and searched. Was she begging on the streets in some other part of the country?

Any night, if Priya listened, he would hear her sobs. They were everywhere; sometimes, like tonight, they would be so close he could almost touch them. At other times, he didn't know which were his sobs and which were hers. When the wind was high, they whimpered and curled into homeless corners.

Even as he tried to shut out the dream of her, he heard a gentle knock on the wooden door. He half sat up and then lay back. It was the wind, playing tricks on his foolish fancies, as his mother would admonish sharply if he were to call to her. But there it was again. He crept up on his hands and knees so as not to awaken the sleeping baby or his mother lying on the other side, and listened with his ear to the door. Then he was on his feet, pulling down the wooden slat that locked it. And there, in the light of the crescent moon, was Mala.

'Amme, amme, our Mala is here,' he yelled back into the house, but his voice, a high treble, was no more than a squeak. 'Mala akka has come home,' he whispered.

He caught hold of her skirt and pulled. But there was no need; there was hardly any resistance. It was as if the wind had gathered force to blow her, like a defenceless leaf, into the room.

Quickly he closed the door on the night.

He twisted his arms around her waist then, and buried his face in her dress. She held him to her, stroking his back and crooning. He pressed himself closer and closer, and then drew back violently. He gazed at her in horror. The hardness of her stomach was unmistakable. Had he not felt it the first time? He shivered. He looked up at her beseechingly. Why, Mala, why again? Didn't she remember how it had been? But he said nothing, and together they looked towards their mother who stirred on her mat and muttered. And when she sat up like she'd seen a ghost, and moaned, 'Mala?' they drew closer to her. Every night, Asilin moaned Mala's name in her sleep. But if Priya dared mention it in the daytime, she would shout at him, 'If she comes within sight of this house, I'll cut her up and throw her in the sea.' Yet she'd look back furtively in the direction of the road. Like Priya she searched the distance for the speck of red that could be Mala's skirt.

Now, Priya switched on the light. Shadows that crouched all over the floor during his long vigils fled to corners. Mala, there was only Mala. Priya never forgot it – the way the light from the naked bulb encircled her there in the centre of the room, and the warmth that radiated from her. But she did not smile, or pull him to her again. She only looked around sullenly.

'Your father's gone to sea,' their mother said, just as sullenly. Now that she knows Mala is safe, she's going to nag her, Priya thought, full of resentment. He drew closer to his sister.

'Go and make us some tea, malli,' Mala said to him, barely looking in his direction. Uncertainly he moved towards the kitchen. But he kept glancing back. He couldn't bear to be away – perhaps she'd disappear again.

He stood at the doorway until the water boiled. She was bent over her baby, her face gaunt and sad. He saw her as more beautiful than the picture of

Mother Mary. The next day he would squat on the wet sand and sketch his sister's face gazing down at the baby. As a wave erased it, he would stare far, far into the distance. And kneeling just there on the sand, palms clasped, he would pray to the gods who controlled their lives.

'Where in God's name have you been, Mala?' asked Asilin. Priya strained his ears for her reply.

'Take that cursed child where you are going, don't leave him behind for us,' his mother said, when Mala still remained silent. Priya cringed at the change in his sister's face.

'Aney amme, do keep quiet,' he pleaded.

When Priya returned with the tea, Mala and his mother were sitting side by side on the floor, leaning against the wall. Asilin was stroking Mala's hair, trying to discipline the long wavy tresses in the old familiar way. It seemed to Priya that his sister had never gone away. He gave them their glasses of tea and scraped half spoons of sugar into their palms. He had also prepared a bottle of plain tea for the baby that he now held to its lips. Mala watched, licking the sugar from her palm between sips of tea. She did not offer to feed the baby. Soon the little sucking lips fell apart, and the baby slept tiredly, its hunger momentarily appeased. As Priya gave Mala the half-empty bottle, he saw her wipe her eyes. He was happy to see her cry. It seemed to him that she might melt that way, with tears, and then she could be the old Mala again, dimpling and laughing and, with side-long glances, flirting with all the young men. How she was changed.

'Go to sleep, malli. Come here, lie against me.' Mala spoke to him at last in the voice he remembered, and happily Priya crawled up to her and lay his head in her lap. As in the old days, he felt her fingers absently ruffling his hair.

'How are the two girls?' Mala asked their mother.

'The good sisters found them a place after they saw what happened to you. They don't get paid much, but they are fed, I think. I go and visit them sometimes,' she replied. Her voice was matter of fact, but Priya knew what it cost her to talk about her children as servants.

'That's good,' Mala murmured. And then, 'You haven't grown at all, you sprat,' she said, bending over him.

'How can he? When that unfortunate pariah of yours drinks up all the money in the house?' Asilin snapped back.

Mala leaned tiredly against the wall. And as she stretched back, their mother suddenly noticed the protrusion of her stomach outlined against her dress. She threw up her arms.

'Mala, again! Oh, you are cursed and so are we. Holy mother of God, let the sea take us all and spare us the shame.'

'Just let me rest a while, amme, I am so tired. So tired. If only you knew.'

'Let her be, will you, amme? Please don't scold her,' Priya said.

'You keep quiet. Who was it this time? Whose child is that now?' his mother demanded.

Priya wanted only to close his ears against the shame and fury in his mother's voice. But there was no shutting it out. And there was the sag of his sister's body as she remembered it all.

'The master of the big house,' she said in a monotone. 'The lady was kind, but I had to leave. I ran away to the girls' home where the convent sent me the last time but I had to come home, amme.'

A long, lonely silence followed. Outside, the wind had changed. It rose and rose and shrieked and howled as it hungered for them all. They heard the coconut fronds tear out and swing down to the ground. Priya thought how he would have to drag them to the back of the house tomorrow, so his mother could weave them for the Sunday fair. Since Mala and the two younger sisters had gone away they had extra work to do, all except their father who sailed to sea every evening, drank toddy every morning, and slept it all away in the afternoon.

Mala sighed heavily. 'We are small fish caught in big nets,' she said hopelessly. How like his mother's voice was his sister's. Priya had not noticed it before. 'If the child lives, and it's a girl, I will call her Kumari. They had a daughter at the big house, and that was her name. She's dead now.'

Heavily the silence fell on them again. Priya lay against Mala. He felt that someone had knifed them all a second time. How could they stop the bleeding again and again? He had no idea who had done it, whether it was his mother or his father or his sister, or the master of the big house, or the baby growing in Mala. What he did know was that one morning he would open the front door to find this next baby on their doorstep, just like the first time.

There would be an uproar. His mother would tear her hair and beat her breasts, flinging curses on Mala and on the father of the infant, and his father would rush up and down the beach with the fish knife, flinging it around and slashing imaginary people, the stale smell of toddy spewing from his breath. All the neighbour women would gather to gossip about Mala and her waywardness. They'd remember how she sauntered past their houses enticing their husbands or their sons to follow her. They'd remember how she'd run back from the sea after a bath, her hair glistening in the evening sun, her breasts half-revealed by the thin bath cloth. And they'd say she deserved what she got . . . And it would be left to Priya to take the baby in his arms, carry it to the bench behind the house and skulk there with it, until it was safe to slink back in. The only difference this time would be that the baby would have a name. And Mala would be sixteen years old, instead of fifteen.

Another baby, he thought, another mouth to feed. He could see his mother, up on the stool, reaching for the broken-handled cup behind the picture of Mary and baby Jesus. Desperately, she'd circle the cup's emptiness with her fingers before turning it upside down, as if it would magically spill a shower of coins on them. Then she'd place it back, clasp her palms together and mutter a prayer to the picture. At last, she'd turn to him and say, 'Mother Mary will look after us.'

But Priya knew better. He'd just have to work twice as hard to contribute to the broken-handled cup. He would return to the cabana at the far end of the beach and go with the white men. Mala had gone to the far end of the beach too. That was what had happened the first time. And that was why the baby was a funny light shade with no-colour eyes. And that's why everyone called it Mala's pariah. Still hurting, he turned his face towards her body, breathing in her smell, her sweat, her cushioning warmth. And then, as if in a dream that only they could share, he felt her hand gently guiding his palm to the side of her stomach. And ever so softly, against her quivering skin, he could feel the tap, tap of the unknown child. Again and again he felt it, and he knew that through him, his sister listened to it too, the fluttering life of the little one.

'If the lady is kind, leave the child at their doorstep, Mala. That's all there is to do. Don't dump it here – your father will kill it.'

Priya closed his eyes and ears. He only wished that he were older, that he had his own place where his sister could have her baby. He began to suck on the knuckle of his thumb. Only twelve years old, and good for nothing, as his mother said.

'. . . don't sew up the mouth of the pillowcase, Mala,' he heard his mother advise Mala between sleep and dream. 'That bodes ill for the mother.' And, '. . . in the last months, remember to throw some paddy seeds to the floor and bend down to pick up the grains one at a time. That way, you won't have too much labour pain. I remember . . .' His sister murmured something in reply. Where would she have the money for pillows and paddy? Their voices dripped with sleepless anguish. And he heard Mala say, perhaps sometime later, 'Aney amme, what is going to happen to me? It was very bad the first time, all alone in the girls' home so far away. The attendants were cruel women . . . I hoped the child would die.'

And again, 'They will not help me at the Corner House, amme. The master didn't even come downstairs when I left. Can't I stay here, at home?'

Much later, Priya awakened fully. He half sat up. His sister lay fast asleep with her head on her mother's shoulder. And the mother sat very straight, the baby in her lap, staring at the picture of Mary and Jesus.

'Are you praying, amme?' he asked timidly.

'No,' she said, without removing her eyes from the picture. 'Your father will be home in an hour or so. It's nearly light. Make more tea, Priya, so your sis-ter can have some before she leaves.'

'Is she leaving?' he asked, dismayed. His mother turned now to cuff him over the ears.

'Must you always ask questions?' she said, but there was no anger in her voice, just that rough and fleeting tenderness that Priya knew so well. They all lived for such moments, but today he was not warmed by it. Her words fell like pebbles into a hollow well.

He wandered away to the kitchen, tears spring-ing to his eyes. He opened the window and peered through the poles. The wind was down. It was going to be a clear day. In the faint light of dawn he could see the backyard strewn with the debris from last night's storm.

Soon they would spot their father's catamaran heading home and his mother would call him to go down by the beach to help haul it in. Priya hoped it would be a good catch this morning.

Mala leaned back against a coconut tree and circled her arms around it in tired abandonment. She moved languorously, seeking comfort against its hardness.

It was a late evening. Passers-by paused inquisitively, whispering to each other. Some stared boldly at the fullness of her body; others smirked suggestively. But Mala's thoughts were focused far out over the sea.

Some small boats were fishing quite close to Lihiniya Island. She saw the flock of birds rise into the air like a dark cloud, and knew they had spotted the fish bubbles. it would be a good night for the fishermen.

This was also the time when the stilt-fishing thieves would zoom in to steal the lihiniya eggs. Her father had taught her never to disturb the eggs of the lihiniya birds. The eggs were full of nutrition, and tasted deliciously of fish, but they were sacred because the lihiniya birds were the faithful guides of the fishermen. She cursed herself, thinking of Neela and Mohan, whom she'd grown to love, and who'd looked after her so well, and how she'd stolen from them their most intimate treasure. She knew she would go to hell for it. She would never have the courage to confess a mortal sin like that to Father Lucien. She knew his faith in her would be lost then, finally.

'Aney aiye, what an unfortunate girl I am, what a sinner . . . ' she moaned. Simon was standing beside her and she turned away, hiding her face from him. 'Has our father gone to sea?' She would make sure of this before beginning to walk down the beach.

How she'd changed from the lovely girl she had been, Simon thought, looking after her. How soon she'd grown old. She had been a lamp, lighting up his house.

In the distance, Priya had his hand raised to her in welcome.

Mala's visits gave Asilin and Priya a bit of respite. She'd sit on the floor, her back against the wall, and place her baby on her stretched-out legs, swaying it to some tune in her head. She'd flick through the paper that their mother collected for wrapping fish and read bits of news aloud in her laboured way, her finger pausing at each word. She showed Priya pictures of Hindi film stars. She cut them out and folded them carefully to take away with her. She was thin and gaunt, but the new baby grew bigger and bigger in her and she grew more and more ungainly. She would often tell Priya to make her a glass of tea with a bit of crushed ginger in it. Some-times Asilin cooked special dishes for her – the white mora, if the net drew it in, for welling up mother's milk. Or lots of tempered keera.

Mala seemed passively unhappy as she sat around the house or on the bench in the backyard, shielded from the neighbours. When the homebound fishing boats glimmered far out at sea, she'd get ready to wander away. Asilin would slide a small packet of last night's rice into Mala's tattered reed bag. God only knows where her next meal is coming from, she muttered. Mala would never say when she would return and Priya grew more and more frightened that one day she would disappear altogether. But Asilin said, 'Oh she'll be back, we know what she's like.' All the same, she would stare anxiously after Mala's retreating figure.

As the weeks passed, Priya and his mother began to heave loud sighs of relief when they saw Mala pushing herself up the beach towards them. Priya would run to her and catch hold of her hand. He'd touch her bulging stomach and ask if the baby had moved. Sometimes she'd smile at him, and Priya's heart filled with joy.

'Anyone would think you were the father, the way you go on about this child,' Mala said, and playfully pulled him close to her.

Held by her like this, Priya suddenly found himself entering a new dream world. And in that world he would be more alone than ever. It was as if she led him to a secret cave and there, on his naked body, plucked a chord of throbbing music.

Confused and frightened, he lagged behind and let her walk on. When he couldn't bear it any more, he ran into the sea and let the waves wash over him. As he surrendered to the moment, he imagined it was night, and that it was a long time ago, and that he lay against the pulse of Mala's baby-coconut breasts.

Simon came out of his house to talk to her. He bent to her face, and drew away a wispy strand of hair from it. She raised her arm and pressed it back in a remembered gesture. Their hands touched, and fell sadly away. Her body leaned backwards to carry the weight of her child.

'Where will you have the baby, Mala? Has the Corner House arranged for it?'

She looked at him sullenly. 'I won't worry you again, aiye, I know our father will kill you if he finds out that you are helping me. You will not find me on your doorstep like the last time.'

Even as he stood helpless by her, he dreamt of the way the years had sped past, wounding her, forcing her away from them. He sensed all those strangers moving in and out of her life. Whose eyes were those unveiling her body with secret desire? Who was that who sought her hand, shielded slightly by the coconut tree? Who was it that moved past her now, blind to her mute despair? Did she remember how he himself had petted her when she was a little girl? And carried her? And made her spin in the wind like a top? Tears seeped into his eyes as he turned away. But Mala's eyes were dry.

'I have to go now, aiye,' she said with tenderness, trying to smile.

He knew she bore him no anger. He felt humbled in her presence.

She stopped returning to the beach after that. The monsoons began to blow and Jamis could not go to sea any more. Again, Simon and Priya went fishing in the lagoon. When Simon got up on the bridge to throw the dulu net in the water, and it sank in a silvery blur, he remembered Mala's lagoon song. And the way they had laughed, the three of them, when she released a puffer fish from the net and held it in her palm until it expanded into a yellow and black ball.

When the full moon waned, Asilin knew that the baby had been born. They waited and waited. Asilin had collected some baby clothes and a new milk bottle, hiding them in the kitchen cupboard for when Mala would be sighted again. But she did not return. Priya combed the beach for her, and Asilin even went to the convent for information. But the sisters shook their heads in resignation. They'd done what they could for Mala. They had inquired at the girls' home where they'd found refuge for her the first time, but this time she'd come and gone sporadically, they said, and no one had seen her lately. The sisters said they'd pray for Mala every night, and asked Asilin to send her to confession if she returned. They still missed her – she had kept the chapel so clean and tidy. But now, what more could they do?

Priya blamed his mother for not making arrangements for Mala's confinement. 'You could have told her to come home to have her baby, amme,' he said.

But half distraught, she shouted back. 'And when your father sees her? Can you shield her from his blows? He'll kill her. Don't you remember the first time?'

Later, they heard something of what had taken place. And they all conjured up their own scene . . .

It happened in a deserted devale just beyond the village, Simon says to Aruni, pointing in that direction. Only the few Hindu Tamil fisher families worshipped in it, in the old days. But then, they were forced to migrate to the East when the war began. After that, except for an occasional devotee, no one visited the devale anymore.

This is where Mala lay. It was pitch-black inside, now that she'd closed the heavy wooden door. She lit a few lamps that still held the dregs of burnt oil. Small flames struggled and sputtered, shedding a faint glow. Smoke rose in frail spirals and spread a musty smell in the airless stone cave. The goddess, once beautiful and commanding, stared down with neglected eyes. Mala sat close to the crevice that at some time in the past had been the home of another statue – perhaps a lesser goddess. When the pain began, she crept into the crevice. Her moans rose into the lonely night. In the wait between, her eyes cleaved to a few flowers that struggled out of the cracks of the crevice. They leaned sideways reaching hopelessly for light. She could make out that they were faintly blue.

'Please, Goddess,' she prayed, 'let this be over soon. I will place these blue flowers at your altar for thanksgiving.' Feverishly, she recited her rosary, and the prayers fell out of her lips in fragments. She clutched the walls and they scoured and bled her fingers. She pulled at the rosary, clenching it in her mouth to stifle the screams. It snapped and a few beads fell on the floor and rolled away. She groped for them as if her life depended on getting them all back. She prayed and cursed and lost all control of her body. She gave birth to a little girl. She picked her up in soiled hands.

'Kumari,' she whimpered holding the infant away from her, 'your father will look after you. And you'll be a lady.'

It was Simon who first heard that Mala had been seen in the devale. When he got to her, she'd already had her baby. Later, he told the family how he'd seen her, crawled tightly into the deep narrow crevice in the wall, her knees folded up, and her arms curled around them. When he flashed his torch on her, she had scraped her nails into the walls trying to creep deeper in. When Simon lifted her out of the crevice she seemed to come alive feebly, and curled into his arms. In the background, the infant whimpered without end. Mala had tried to appease the goddess with marigolds that had shed their petals of gold through the long night. Much later, with her feeble help, he cleaned the floor with rags.

Mala refused to be taken home and wanted no one to know where she was. The next day Simon came back with food for her, and ginger tea in his flask. But she had already gone by then, with the baby, leaving behind nothing but the blood that had seeped into the cracks of the crevice. He sat on the steps knowing she would not return. He threw the rice he had cooked for her to the stray dogs, and emptied the flask of tea onto the sand.

'I knew I would not see her again,' Simon says to Aruni.

He returns exhausted to her from the distant memory. He sees the frozen tears melt and spill out, at last. She clutches at his hand.

'I told you to leave us alone,' he says. He gets up and walks into his house, closing the door behind him.

When Aruni looks up at last, she finds Priya in Simon's chair. She raises her eyes to his. He moves his hand finally, across the years, and touches the wetness on her cheek.

Aruni sits in her window seat staring out to sea. Paul reads nearby. It's long past midnight, but he is reluctant to suggest that they sleep. She seems so vulnerable tonight, consumed by the unwinding of her mother's life and the story of her own birth.

'I might go to bed then, Aruni. I'll see you in the morning?'

She turns slowly. 'What's that you're reading?' she asks, and her voice is tired and drained.

'The Bible. I found it in the drawer – they're desperate for converts.' Paul grimaces, trying to inject some lightness. He's glad she's responding to something at last.

'You don't believe in religion, Paul. Why are you reading the Bible?'

It's a beautiful story, he says, don't you know that? Read me a bit then, she says. If only he could give her the gift of faith in humanity. He turns the pages slowly, draws up to her and reads of the birth of Moses. And as she turns to stare out of the window again, she sees in the night's luminous depths, the sacred manifestation of motherhood.

And the woman conceived, and bore a son; and when she saw he was a goodly child, she hid him three months.
And when she could no longer hide him, she took for him an ark of bulrushes, and daubed it with slime and with pitch and put the child therein; and she laid it in the flags by the river's brink.
And the daughter of Pharoah came down . . . and when she saw the ark among the flags she sent her maid to fetch it. And when she opened it, she saw the child; and behold, the babe wept. And she had compassion for him . . .

Paul closes the book and switches off the lamps in the room. They sit in the darkness most of the night. Off and on, he hears her stir. He bends forward to settle her pillow behind her head. In the morning he wakes her with a cup of hot tea. She opens her eyes. He holds the cup to her lips. With her fingers on his hand, and with the beginnings of a smile, she drinks.

When Neela found the sleeping baby on her doorstep, she bent towards it with a rapturous smile. It was almost as if she had known this day would happen, that the dream would one day continue into life. There was no surprise in the expected. She felt the baby's small body beneath the cloth wrapped around it and crooned to it. She waited for the remembered dimples.

'Mohan, look,' she murmured, 'Kumari is returned to us!'

She looked for him, wondering why he was not bending over her to welcome back their daughter. For a moment more she lived in the cherished dream. She went down on her knees, drawing the infant into her arms, and it was only then that she saw the piece of paper pinned on to the cloth. Even as she unfolded it, a few crushed blue flowers fell out. Neela smelt their funeral smell.

She read the brief note. She drank the poisoned truth.

She looked out over the baby into the familiar garden and saw it draining of colour. She saw all the blues and reds and yellows seep into the flowers she crushed in her palm. She stared down at them. They burned in her palm like lighted jewels. The tears came then, blurring the blue, and she knew the flowers were inextricably pressed into her life. She picked the baby out of the box and carried her into the house. She laid her in the middle of the double bed and sat beside her until she heard old Menika calling from the hall. Drearily she returned to life. She folded the flowers back into Mala's letter and placed the paper in the almirah. She left it where Mohan would find it . . .

She sat at the dressing table. In the mirror she watched Mohan unfold the note and read it. If there was a spark of hope deep within her, it did not reveal itself on her face. She saw him look up from the note and turn swiftly towards her. Their eyes met in the mirror. There was terrible confusion in his gaze, the yearning to be released from guilt. It was a begging look. But she saw nothing but the treachery behind it. She could not release him. She remembered how she had loved him with so much more than the respect of a wife for a husband. She remembered how safe she had felt wrapped up in his tenderness. The night their daughter had been conceived – the joyful lovely dream. And she hated him for what he had carelessly thrown away. She was violated. This was, for her, their moment of parting.

There had been no need for the letter because, as soon as he had seen the baby, he had understood. He had only wanted to spare her the knowledge. It was even a relief that he did not need to harbour the dreadful secret any longer. He placed the note back under the paper and moved away. Neela saw him step carelessly on the bruised blue flowers that had fallen out, and she began to sob, wracking sobs that seemed to empty the room in which they had consecrated their love. She rushed to pick up the flowers, clutching them in her hand. She did not know what she could do with them.

Neela and Mohan never discussed the truth. They kept the child, but knew she would always come between them. They tried to meet across a space that was too wide, too deep. When they talked together of her, they referred to her as Mala's daughter. And for Neela, in her deepest thoughts, Aruni remained Mala's daughter. But for Mohan? Occasionally, when he bent to lift her out of the cradle, in her beautiful large eyes he saw Mala. He jumped back, as if restless spirits hovered on his grave. At other times, he'd pick her up and croon Mala's song to her. As Aruni grew up, it became their song, exclusively and privately theirs. A song in which Neela had not a line. Not a single note. A song she absorbed with all the sadness with which it was sung. And the secrets it held.

Mohan sat at the piano for long hours in the night. His fingers touched the keys and his voice spread into all the cracks in the house.

He was lost between one birth and the next. He couldn't find the way. He met a butterfly and she led him to her dreamland. She enclosed him in it for a while. He asked her the way, but she couldn't reply. She smiled into the wind her knowledge and her lack of it. She spread her wings and fluttered away. He wondered why they had met. He tried to follow her but she flew away. Passing from one birth to the next, he asked the way from a butterfly that did not know its way.

Neela lived through to the end of the song. She got out of bed and stood by the window. She gazed out into the garden where Mala had sat night after night, combing down her long hair, drenched in moonlight, her song wafting warmly into their room, melting the silences.

In appreciation of the new baby, they gave an alms-giving for mothers. The women came in before dawn, dressed in white and exuding all the purity of mother-hood. As they entered the house, Neela washed their feet with saffron water. She welcomed them to the mat laid out in the hall, served them food and offered them clothes. She brought out the child and displayed her to the women. She did all according to custom and ritual. Mohan shared it with her. But when the women went to the kitchen area after the almsgiving, to gossip a bit with Menika, she felt full of hypocrisy. She felt that the Goddess Pathini, to whom they had given blessings for the new daughter this morning, must know the truth and curse the charade of the almsgiving. Neela bent over the baby fearfully. It looked back at her unsmiling, without recognition. She handed her over to Mohan, and walked wearily upstairs. She lay down in the bed, her eyes on the photograph on the side table, of herself, Mohan and the dead daughter.

So they proclaimed to the world their claim on Aruni. Privately, they drew up her adoption papers. They went together to the Mt Lavinia District Court to sign them. They sat side by side on the row of seats allocated to would-be parents and stared at the opposite row, at the mothers who were giving their babies away for adoption. There they sat, the young girls, in their ill-fitting dresses, holding malnourished infants. They gazed vacantly at nothing in particular. Older women sat with some of them looking angry or hopeless or just resigned. Two ceiling fans, grey and dusty, whirled around in the airless room, making a creaking sound as if they would break free any moment from their sockets. Mohan kept looking up at them, and wiping the sweat off his forehead. He wore a dark blue shirt and it showed wet patches. Neela looked down at the child and realised she was clutching her tightly. She gave her to Mohan and stepped out of the room. The afternoon heat was intense. Crows perched here and there in the shade. She watched a lonely girl-mother buy a bottle of orange barley from the cart vendor, and the way she drank off the bottle while the baby's head drooped at her shoulder. When the girl passed by her to return to the room, Neela smiled slightly. The girl went in, her expression stony and withdrawn. Perhaps she did it for the money, Neela thought, tiredly taking her seat again.

Neela struggled to accept that Aruni was Kumari reborn to them. She blocked out the rest. She feared that she had yearned for her so passionately that the child's spirit had been unable to rest, and had been lured back. But Neela could not love her. Not the way she had loved Kumari with that ineffable mother love. And when Aruni opened her piercing black eyes it seemed she was aware of this, and Neela felt an endless guilt and remorse, and scooped the baby into her arms.

'Kumari,' she whispered against her will but with a nascent tenderness, 'Kumari, my daughter.'

She felt Mohan's presence in the room. He came up close and bent over her shoulder.

'No, Neela, let the other one rest. Let us call her Aruni – Aruni – dawn. Let her begin a new life for both of us.'

Neela turned then, slightly, towards him, and their eyes fluttered, fled away and met at last. His lips brushed her forehead over the new promise. It was a pledge of fidelity, a plea for forgiveness. It meant that he would acknowledge the child not as his, but theirs. He opened his arms wide and wanted to hold her to him, baby and all. But she only saw that he held out his arms over the grave of their daughter. The chasm was too wide, too deep, to be crossed. She cast down her eyes. She tried not to remember that this was Mohan's child, not hers. She held the child passionately, with desperate hope, and she felt her breasts swell, as if milk were welling up in them. In a haze, she opened her blouse and held the baby to her breast. But the baby turned away and began to whimper. Her exposed breast, empty and hard, stared down at the child with a cold censoring eye. Mohan's face clouded with sorrow. Shame spilt out of his eyes. He backed away from the scene.

Finally, Priya and his mother came to the Corner House. They were desperate for news of Mala. Months had gone by without a word or a sign. They stood at the heavy iron gates and peered in. Stretching to his full height, Priya pushed back the latch. They entered the garden and walked up the drive to the front doorsteps. Priya let his fingers trace the side of the shiny black car parked in the porch.

Neela opened the door. She held the baby in her arms.

'It is Mala's mother, hamu,' Asilin said. 'Is this her child?' She crept closer. Neela's face registered shock. Quickly she stepped back, trying to hide the baby in the folds of her dress. She withdrew into the house and asked Menika to take the baby upstairs for her bath. When she saw that Menika was out of the way she came back and invited Asilin and her son to the back entrance.

'Mala is not here, she did not come back. Here, you can take her clothes away,' she said coldly, and thrust a brown paper bag at Asilin.

But Asilin drew away and it was left to Priya to take the bag. He looked in it, and smelt his sister's smell on her clothes. It enveloped his senses and he stared past Neela into the kitchen area as if he was sure his sister was hidden within. Now she would appear, he thought, now she would come swaying out in that saucy way she had, and rumple the hair that he'd pasted down with oil.

'Aney hamu, the girl never came home to have her baby. That is why we came looking for her here. We have been everywhere else.' Asilin slid down on the doorstep, her hands raised in suppliance.

But Neela stood tall and proud and unrelenting, barring the doorway.

'Here is some money,' she said, holding out more than Priya had ever seen before. 'Take it and go away, please. Please don't bother us any more. Your daughter left months ago and never returned. We informed the convent at the time. We are not responsible for her.'

Asilin was past weeping. She shrivelled and shrank into herself. Against her will, Neela recognised the pain of lost motherhood, and turned into the kitchen.

'I will get you a cup of tea, amme,' she said.

Priya felt nothing but a cold and empty space within him. He knew it would never end. His sister was lost, and he would wait and wait, and he would never see her again. He stumbled towards the edge of the garden, choking on his sobs. His shoulders heaved. There was a small bench by the jak tree. He was about to sit on it when he saw a small mirror on a wooden shelf nailed to the tree. He reached up and discovered on the shelf, Mala's old comb and a photograph wrapped up tightly in a bit of cellophane. He pulled out the photograph with trembling fingers. It was of his sister, holding the half-caste in her arms and leaning slightly towards him. She smiled out of the picture now, as if she and Priya shared a secret. The sky was a wonderful blue behind them.

– Anyone would think you were the father of this baby, his sister said.

He pushed the comb and the photograph into his shirt pocket and stretched further for anything else that might be lying forgotten. His fingers closed around a sliver of cracked soap. He turned it in his palm. It was wet with the night's rain, and slippery, almost as if Mala had just used it, and wanted him to share it with her. Priya lifted it to his nose and inhaled, but it was not the smell of his sister. This was a soft fragrant soap, a lady's soap. How she must have loved using it, relishing its smooth softness on her skin. But perhaps she had stolen it from the lady. He cringed, imagining spying eyes and the heaviness of a hand descending on his shoulder, catching him out with stolen goods. Somehow, he did not want this remnant of his sister. He threw it with all his might into the patch of vegetables nearby. As he turned to return to his mother, he looked up at the house.

He saw Mohan at the window upstairs, holding the baby. Even as their eyes met across the garden, Mohan moved back into the room. If Priya had been a braver boy, he'd have aimed a stone at the window. As it was, he just stared in dismay at the big house – it looked to him like the Welikada Jail that he had once visited with Simon, when their father had been shut up there.

He went up to his mother.

'Let's go, amme,' he said, 'there is nothing in this house for us. Let's buy our tea from the tea butik on the roadside.' He took his mother's arm and helped her to her feet.

'But the baby, they have our Mala's baby,' she said.

'They will bring it up, amme, and they won't let you have it now.' He did not remind his mother that it was she who had ordered Mala to give up the baby to this house. Or perhaps he did not remember right – he had been half asleep when the words had crossed between his mother and his sister.

'She's dead, our Mala is dead,' Asilin began to repeat to herself as if she were reciting the rosary. She walked where Priya led her, senselessly. They went around the house. Priya left the gate open. He hoped that the demon spirits hovering around would creep into the house through all the cracks in the walls. He took a fistful of sand, as he had seen his father do, and, blowing into it, cursed all the people who would tread the soil of that garden. He threw the sand at the gate. He did not know what else he could do to stop the bleeding of his mother's heart.

Neela watched the woman and the boy walk away. She saw the boy throw the sand at the gate. It was only what was deserved. She emptied the tea from the glasses and washed them. She wiped her hands and turned to return upstairs to her husband and baby. But the steps were too high.

She walked all around the house, and ended up in Mala's room behind the kitchen. She felt herself locked in this house, isolated as in a high tower that let in no air. Life was ever deepening silence. She sat down on the edge of the narrow bed that Mala had slept on, and turned to the window. Slowly, without thinking, she lay back against the pillow. It seemed to her that Mala's smell was still on it, and on the sheets. On the wall, a calendar held the naïve face of a Hindi film star. Mala had circled dates on it. Neela wondered what they meant, and could not guess. On the windowsill, a long strand of black hair. It curled around her finger like a living thing. We nurtured a venomous serpent in our house, she thought.

When Neela was still unmarried, a cobra had lain on the front doorstep of their walauwa. Her mother had placed a saucer of milk every morning for it, and watched with tenderness as it was lapped up. Her mother had believed the cobra was the spirit of some dead beloved that had returned to protect their home. But her father had always been suspicious of it, and had driven it away before it weaved its insidious venom into the house. People who nurture a serpent in their house have only themselves to blame, he had said roughly to her mother, who for months had sat listless on the step seeking its return.

Neela thought of how Mala had sat on this bed, night after night, combing down her sinuous hair. She remembered Mohan coming out of this room one evening, with a glass of iced water, and how he'd said that Mala looked as if she were entombed in an ektamge, awaiting her lover whom she would lure in. Neela tried to remember the tone of his voice, but failed. Perhaps he and Mala shared their first intimacies in this room? Had she caught his hand and smiled with him with her long serpent eyes? Why had Neela not suspected any of this? How naively she had trusted him. How sacred had been that trust. Was it Mala's song that had lured Mohan to her body? Had he come to her here in the nights? Her eyes searched with frantic pain for fragments he might have left behind. If only she could understand how or why or what could have happened. But there was no other evidence. She fixed her gaze once more outside the window. She saw white clouds. As they shaped and reshaped and shaped again, she saw Kumari in her arms. There was Mohan with them, and then like a shadow consuming the silvery translucence of the formation, Mala. For a moment, shot through with intense light, Neela saw her husband turn and reach for the girl, and the sordid embrace. She saw her daughter's eyes transfixed on the intense rhythm of the moment. She forced the child's face into the safe soft womb. And then they all faded out. Neela turned into the pillow.

When she looked out of the window again, the sky stretched in one colourless cloud. She was still there when Menika walked in. She sat up then, tidying her hair. Harshly, she ordered Menika to clear out Mala's bed and dust out the room. 'I was going to do it, hamu, I just had no time,' the old woman apologised, with a surprised look at her mistress. 'I will do it now, Aruni baba is asleep upstairs.'

Late, late in the sleepless nights, Neela wept to Mohan's music. It floated up to her in waves of tenderness. He sang of their child, and of her premature death. He sang of her milk-tasting breath and her bright eyes. And as they carried her to her grave, wrapped all in white, he pleaded with the gods that flowers of restfulness might blossom on her grave.

Neela turned to Mohan in an aggression born of despair. He submitted timidly, yearning only to comfort her, to make their world secure again. The past dissolved and waveringly receded. And the stars flashed with a brilliance that lighted up the room, and the night burned to their passion. And when it was over, he held her with renewed tenderness. He gazed around gratefully and felt the walls strong once more. Their home would continue as before. But even as he dreamt his dream, she withdrew into her silent world.

She wondered yet again, as she turned to her side and faced the wall, how it had been for him with Mala. Had he, in the deepest moments when he was locked into her, imagined she was the servant girl who slept in the back room? Mala with her flaunting beauty, her thick ugly lips, and coarse dark body? Does he still feel and smell the heart of her poisoned flower? Suddenly the bed was full of the smell of the other woman, it swirled around the room in a large nebulous net, and netted her in, until she screamed to be released. The night reverberated to the sound of sobs and there was no knowing whose they were, or who stifled them.

Aruni was a small secretive thing. When visitors came to the house, she stood in corners or behind doors and stared at them until they felt uncomfortably that perhaps their hair was not combed quite right, or that their sari was falling off. Menika said that when Aruni slept she dreamt with her eyes. The lids quivered and the half-opened eyes rushed around as if in search of some secret. She knew she did not belong in the house; she sensed a secret surrounding her birth.

There were pictures of her sister Kumari that she was not allowed to touch. Not a day went by without Menika or her mother mentioning the dead sister's name. Every year, on the night before Kumari's birthday, Menika and Neela cooked alms.

There would be thirteen monks for this almsgiving, one for every year of Kumari's life had she lived. Many relatives came to the house before the monks were escorted in. Some of the ladies went at once into the kitchen to help out. After the food had been served to the monks, the chief monk blessed the house and its inhabitants and said that the dead daughter had received the merits that were offered her through the clergy. As he was leaving, Neela paid him obeisance, touching the floor at his feet. The monk said that she was attaining great merit by the way she remembered the dead child. Little Aruni hid behind her, and listened.

After all the visitors had departed, Neela sat under the rambutan tree with Aruni. Menika brought her a cup of tea. Neela and Menika talked desultorily about the almsgiving, comparing it to the year before.

'If only Kumari baba had not been taken away from us, she would be having a party not an almsgiving,' Menika murmured.

Neela's eyes turned inward with naked pain, and excluded Aruni sitting on her lap. Aruni put her arms around Neela and assured her in her most passionate voice that she loved Kumari akki just as her mother and Menika and her father did. And that she missed her too. But Neela lifted Aruni out of her lap and withdrew into a place that she could not enter.

Aruni's room was next to that of her parents. In the depths of the night she awakened to the sound of her father's voice downstairs. A soft breeze played in the room, stirring up shadows. She heard the ominous call of the devil bird. She knew her mother hated it. Menika said that just the day before her sister Kumari was run over by the lorry, the devil bird had visited their house and flown round and round the hall, knocking against walls. It had entered the house to carry away Kumari's spirit. Her mother swore that she'd heard it for weeks after the cremation. It was like the scream of a bereaved mother, Neela said. And Menika said that the silence that followed was deathly, as if a tortured child had been strangled. Aruni drew herself up into a tight ball now, thinking that devil bird would swoop in any minute to pluck her spirit from her body. She waited and waited, terror spilling out of her staring eyes. But devil bird did not come for her.

Hugging her pillow, she crept out of bed and

tiptoed to her mother. But Neela was asleep. Aruni tugged her arm softly, still frightened and wanting to cuddle in the big bed. But Neela only moaned in her sleep. 'Kumari,' she heard her whisper, 'Kumari, climb into bed, my little duwa, you've returned to us. It was all a bad dream.' Aruni stared emptily. When she was smaller, she had loved being told that she was a good girl like Kumari. But little by little she grew to hate the comparisons. Once, when Menika had called her Kumari baba by mistake, Aruni rushed at her and pummelled her. Menika said later that it would have been the end of her had Aruni seen a knife nearby, so red and insane were her eyes. She'd rolled on the floor and howled until her mother closed her ears in despair and helplessness.

'I am not Kumari. Kumari is dead, dead, dead!'

But now Aruni did not howl. She was a year older and more silently composed. Her eyes grew old in her small pinched face. She looked towards her father's side of the bed and it was empty. She stood undecided for a moment in her long white night-dress, a desolate ghost. Then she heard her father's voice floating up to her from the great cavern of the stairwell. Slowly, trailing her pillow, she went down to him. She climbed into his lap. He continued to sit at the piano and sing his plaintive tune. She knew the song. She sang along with him.

He leaned forward to turn a page, and she felt the rough stubble of his chin. Reaching back, she placed her palms against his cheeks. If she held them a moment longer, she'd have felt the wetness on them. The song was too sad, he thought, the child must go back to sleep in a happy mood. He began to play 'Chopsticks'. She joined in smartly with her fore-fingers. They began to laugh as they played louder and louder, faster and faster.

And to this laughing sound, Neela awakened. She half sat up, then lay back. She turned towards the photograph on the side table and, yet again, she recalled his betrayal. How easily he had forgiven him-self. He must not be allowed to forget. She revelled in his guilt, but sorrowfully. He had violated both her and their dead daughter. And now he sang with his other child, she thought, moaning with excruciating pain, this other child who was not hers, who would never be hers, but was his. She could see them blend, excluding her. She yearned to belong. She knew they would welcome her into their world. And that it was she who could not cross over, could not reach out, could not forgive. She had known that for a long time. And slowly, quietly, without anyone actually feeling it, Mohan had begun to let go, and move on alone. And she? She still grasped and clutched. But knew the bond was slackened.

She suddenly pushed aside the covering sheet and got out of bed. She leaned over the banister. 'Will you stop that noise? Do you know the time? Aruni, it's a school day tomorrow. Mohan, will you let the child sleep?'

She heard her voice, harsh and out of control, echoing in the sudden hush. She heard Mohan close the piano lid. She knew Aruni would be sliding off the edge of the stool that she had shared with him.

Downstairs, they were silenced. They looked at each other. Mohan tried to smile. He saw Aruni's face close up angrily. He bent forward and touched her cheek. But she turned away, resentful that her mother could so control their life together. She rushed up the stairs and brushed past her mother.

'Goodnight, Aruni,' Neela said with a touch of remorse. But Aruni did not reply. She ran into her room.

Neela did not wait for Mohan to come up the stairs. Wearily, she went back to bed. She turned away from the light seeping into the room from the roadside lamp. Loneliness: crouching and leaping, crouching and leaping. Neela drew her arm against her face. Shutting it out, shutting out all seven years of Aruni.

Mohan hesitated at the threshold. His mood had changed quite swiftly to guilt and sorrow. He went to his daughter's room but did not enter it. He returned to Neela. He looked at her a moment, and sighed. She pretended to sleep. He lay down on the other side, his face to the wall.

They lay awake, remembering other nights, another child lying between them. And his voice, singing to her a lullaby. And she would pat the child to his song, smiling with him in the dark.

Aruni walked between Mohan and Neela along the railway line. She jumped from sleeper to sleeper hanging on to their hands. She looked up into their faces often, wanting them to share the excitement of her small clever leaps and balances. But they looked ahead, deadly silent with each other. Lost in their separate thoughts, hardly aware of her. She got frightened of the silence. She tried to join their hands, just to see them smile together. But though they each looked down at the joined hands, and smiled with her, they freed their hands from the forced clasp, and went back into their walled-in selves.

When they returned, Aruni walked upstairs and into her room. Of course, it had been Kumari's room too. And there was dead Kumari smiling down from the walls. As usual, she chatted with Kumari for a while, showing her a flower she'd picked specially for her. She helped Kumari step out of the picture. They sat together and played with their dolls. She wound up her favourite drum-playing teddy and turned it towards Kumari. 'There,' she said, 'that's nice, isn't it? Now you sit there and listen.' But then, on this day, for no reason at all, she got tired of Kumari not replying to her. She pushed the teddy forward. But still Kumari did not respond. She leaned forward and tried to shake her. But there was no one to shake. It was then that she first realised it was all a game. She put her dolls away. She felt lonely now that she knew, too lonely to cry. She leaned down the banister, wondering what to do now she couldn't find her dead sister any more.

And then she heard her parents arguing downstairs. She didn't even try to listen. It happened so often. In a few minutes, her mother would run up the stairs and fall into her bed, weeping into her pillow. Then the car would start up and her father would speed away. She got into her own bed. She must have slept. All around her she saw those ghosts that Menika talked about – they hopped into the room through the window, their bodies hairy and horrible. Menika said they were the spirits of dead people who could not find peace, and so took up residence in a living body. She said it was what a caterpillar did. When it got to the end of one leaf, it stretched out and moved onto another one.

Now Kumari's ghost tried to seep into Aruni. She thrashed around trying to drive it away. But it persisted. Now she would not be Aruni any more, but Kumari. That's what happened when a spirit possessed you. Aruni began to turn violent, still fighting Kumari. Her body shook and spit drooled from her lips. She leapt around, her eyes on fire, her voice rising to a hysterical shriek. But Kumari kept invading her. Then she rolled on the floor, screaming that she was not Aruni any more, but Kumari, Kumari, Kumari.

Menika reached her before her mother did. She caught hold of the maddened child who rushed at her with clenched fists. Menika was feeble with age. It took a long time, but Menika crooned and murmured in her unintelligible way until Aruni had calmed and lay sobbing in her lap. And all this happened while her mother stood by the door. When she saw that Aruni had quietened down, Neela walked away.

It took a long time for any of them to be normal again. Aruni could not be sent to school. She went mute for weeks, and would stand around the house facing walls and trying to get as close as possible to them. All Kumari's photographs were removed and, with nothing to take their place, the house was filled with emptiness. In the nights, when she thought the house was asleep, Aruni got out of her bed, and sat on her small chair with her face to the wall, mumbling confused words. She rocked back and forth on the chair until, awakened by the sound, Mohan came over to carry her back to bed. He lay beside her, his hand on her forehead, singing to her. But she got tired of the hand that had no healing power, and pushed him away. Finally, Neela took Aruni to the temple and had a pirith thread tied round her wrist for protection.

'Not much changed in Australia. We carried all our problems over there. But then, I guess I grew up. I miss my father, though . . .' Aruni says. 'See why I had to come back to where I belong? Think it's been a healing process, Paul?'

Paul says yes. He wonders how much he himself has contributed to her reconstruction. It had all started out so whimsically for him, a live-for-the-moment thing. But he had not expected to feel like this. He wonders how she would react if he took her hand now and told her that perhaps he was beginning to fall in love with her, that his marriage meant nothing, their age difference even less. What if he asked her to go back with him to Australia? Told her that he'd be her friend and her lover and her father, and anything else she wanted him to be? But the moment passes. He gets out of his chair, hurriedly.

'I'm going for a short walk before dinner, Aruni. I'll see you in a bit,' he says casually.

'OK then,' Aruni replies, removing her eyes from his. She says she'll probably just lie there and soak up the evening sun. She pulls out her earphones. But as soon as he turns away, she raises her face, and looks after him. She thinks, that, yes, their journey together is ending. She thinks of all the nights and days that had followed their first chance encounter. She tries to work out details, a look in his eyes, a smile, a touch that showed she meant more to him than a holiday in the sun. But she feels immature and silly. She has no prior knowledge with which to make judgements. Perhaps his whole married life has been travelling around the world having casual flings with younger women who meant nothing to him. It was only her foolish ungrown-up self that had fantasised it was something else – like love, or belonging, or something like that. All her life she had demanded impossibilities – from her mother, from her father, girls at school. But they all had their private lives that excluded her. Now, at eighteen, she should know better. And she does. But there is hurt in her thoughts, and it draws tears. She watches Paul out of sight and goes to sit on the ledge.

And she sees Premasiri on the beach. Her eyes begin to fill with flowers, like crystal vases. She watches him jogging along the edges of the waves. He wears a pair of running shorts, and as he swings his arms in tune with his legs, she sees his skin stretched on taut muscles. He raises his face to the wind and savours it. She playfully does the same. He runs his fingers through his hair. She does the same. She watches him stop and pick something up. She wants to know what it is, and waves to him. He comes up and climbs the ledge until his face is level with hers. She asks him to sit beside her, but no, he says he wants no trouble with the security guards.

He shows her a young coconut that has been tossed about in the sea. 'It's been in the sea for over a week, missy,' he says to her. 'Look, feel the husk, how the hardness has worn away, leaving it soft and mushy. If you reach right into it, the kernel will be as soft as a woman's sex.'

His voice is soft and caressing, his laugh meaningful. She raises her eyes to his and fleetingly drinks in his message. He holds the soft wet fruit to her on his palm. She presses a finger into it. He pushes her finger further and further in, slowly. Salt water, thick as juice, oozes out.

'There,' he says, 'we've sucked it dry.' He swings his arm and throws the coconut back towards the sea. It falls with a heavy thud on the sand. 'The tide will fill her up again,' he says, his eyes inching over her face.

Aruni smiles uneasily. She is still too close to what happened before, with Paul. She sighs deeply, suppressing a sob. But she also laughs and tosses her hair. Leaning over the wall Premasiri touches her eyelashes, all wet and entangled. She lets him smooth them out, and moves her face against the roughness of his fingers.

'I like your hair, missy, it's beginning to grow. You don't look like a porcupine any more.'

'No?' she asks, burying the sob for later. 'What do I look like now, Premasiri?'

Her accent still makes him smile. He tells her what she wants to hear. 'You look like one of us now.'

'Look like? But I am one of you. I've told you that. My mother –'

'Oh yes,' he says, 'we all know that story. But

you are not a beach girl, missy, you will never really be one of us.'

'Maybe you are related to me,' Aruni persists, suddenly serious. 'Aren't all beach families related to each other? Maybe I should call you Premasiri aiya?'

'Oh no,' he laughs uproariously. 'My friends will make such fun of me, missy. I beg of you, don't even mention it.'

Aruni continues to smile and toss her hair. But a new hurt lurks behind her eyes now. She just doesn't want him to see it.

'One of these days,' he says nonchalantly, jumping back to the beach, 'you and Paul sir must come in the glass-bottom boat with us. We'll show you those turtles. They are really something to see. All tourists go for them. We'll give you a special price, missy.'

'You'll have to take me alone, Premasiri. Paul will be going home in a week or two. He has finished his work here.'

After leaving Aruni, Paul walks aimlessly along the beach towards the fishing village. He is subconsciously aware that he is looking for Simon – to tell him that he will be going away soon. But there is only Priya in Simon's chair, minding the kurumba. Priya cuts one and gives it to Paul. He offers Priya a cigarette. He notices the tremor of Priya's fingers as he lifts it to his lips.

Squatting beside the chair, Paul begins to drink. He is quite used to these silences. With a small smile he remembers Aruni and her ancient mariner. He wishes she were with him now. He decides to finish his kurumba and continue on his walk like a sensible tourist. You bought favours from these beach people – a woman, a bit of hashish, a drink – but you didn't make friends with them. And without Aruni, he is just a tourist on the beach.

Priya does not try to keep him. He is floating on his dreams when Paul stands up, pays for his kurumba and goes. But Paul feels Priya's eyes on him, and wonders how safe it really is on this beach at this time of evening. He takes his wallet out of his hip pocket and pushes it behind the belt. He walks without direction, in an inexplicably vague mood. In transit, he thinks, between lands and oceans, between past and present, present and future, between relationships. Whither now, willy nilly blowing, he wonders, picking up a small conch shell and holding it to his lips. It gives back Aruni's taste and her scent. But the shell holds secrets that he cannot reach. The sun is setting. Let's make a wish, Aruni would say, taking his hand in hers, pressing a kiss into it and folding his fingers over it. He turns back to the hotel.

He sees her at the ledge and is about to go up to her when he sees she is not alone. He observes Premasiri draw close to Aruni, and the way his handsome features are absorbed in what she does and says. She seems aflame, touched by the aftermath of the crimson sunset. Paul stares spellbound. In the cocoon of light, no longer distinguishable in themselves, they celebrate a communion beyond his understanding. He moves quietly away.

'Où est la petite fleur?' asks the Frenchman, laying down his daily flower offering for Aruni on the dining table. Paul pretends to be preoccupied in the darkness gathering outside. The light is soon gone from the sky. Aruni and Premasiri are silhouettes, and, from this distance, they seem joined in embrace. The waiter brings him a bowl of water so he can wash his fingers before eating, but perversely he takes up his fork and knife. Not having rice and curry tonight, sir? The waiter hovers. He glances at his friends, smirking slightly. They've seen Aruni flirting with the beach boy down by the ledge. Paul ignores them and orders a drink. The waiter lights the candle on the table. Waiting for his drink, Paul picks up the flower and absentmindedly fiddles with it. It falls apart in his hand. He looks at it sadly. He tries to recall its local name, but it eludes him. In a little while, Aruni comes in and, without looking in his direction, walks off swiftly towards the bedrooms.

After dinner, Paul takes a turn in the garden. He wanders up to the ledge and stares out at the first stars trembling awake. He turns back and pauses at the globes of golden light that he's begun to take for granted. They shine on, indifferent to him, to her, to the world. They'd go shining for a hundred years more, for all us tourists in transit. Perhaps, he thinks, staring into their beautiful glow, perhaps he has been a moment in her growing, in her unravelling. And that was as it should be. He wipes his face with his palms and is surprised to feel the wetness.

Almost out of habit, on the way to his room, he looks in on her. She's left the door ajar. She's waiting for him then, in spite of everything. He smiles and tenderness rushes over him. But she is asleep, the earphones plugged on. He bends over her and gently lifts one earphone and puts it to his own ear. As always, the raucous sounds split his brain. He sits by her and struggles to connect with her world – violent, swearing, rocking. He removes the earphones, bends to kiss her forehead. She stirs slightly, the kiss hovers but does not touch. He draws the sheet around her. Tomorrow, he thinks, tomorrow he will tell her that he'll be leaving for Australia in about a week's time. And she can come with him – or not.

p a r t   t h r e e

The beach boys came for Aruni in the night. She was still asleep when they began to throw small shells at her window. She awakened drowsily, turned her head slowly towards the window. Her eyelids drooped. But her body came alive, soaked in sweat. She drew her palm against her neck and down her breasts, and stretched. She felt a little drunk on nights like this. Like after toddy. She began to listen to the night waves flinging against rock, and to the wind rushing around like a wild lost thing.

But they would not let her be. She walked to the window sleepily, holding the sheet against her. She spotted the silhouettes of three or four men, like shadows lurking behind the coconut trees.

'A turtle, missy,' said one of them in a loud whisper as she opened the window. 'It's a turtle laying eggs on the beach, very close. You always wanted to see that. Come, come quickly, it will be gone in a short while. Paul sir is already there.'

Aruni leaned forward now, fully awake, smiling gleefully. She had waited long for this.

'Missy, missy, come quick.' She heard Premasiri and saw him waving his arms high in the air to claim her attention.

There was no time to dress properly and, on the run, she wrapped a beach cloth carelessly around herself.

She rushed out, and almost into their arms. She saw Premasiri and laughed excitedly, but he had already turned towards the beach. Tucked up against thighs, white sarongs gleamed as bodies clustered around her. There was hardly any moon. It suddenly flashed in Aruni's mind that turtles by habit laid eggs on full-moon nights, and that was why the eggs were so exposed to thieves. She began to voice the thought, but it seemed to vanish into the night. They hurried her along. She winced as something pricked her underfoot. Caught up in their hurry, she began to run, taking long leaping strides along the wet sand. The

236

beach cloth, held by the wind, now clung to her body, now swept away from it. She tried to wrap it close but it seemed to have a teasing life of its own and flirted with the wind. She tried to forget it.

The beach was deserted.

'Where is Paul?' she asked, suddenly alerted. 'Paul,' she called loudly. 'Paul?'

But in the silence that surrounded the moment, she could not hear his voice. She turned to the men.

'He must have gone away, tired of waiting. We told you to hurry. Even the turtle seems to have disappeared,' Premasiri said.

He would not meet her eyes. She was slowly beginning to feel fear. She looked before and behind her. There was no one, no one but the men who seemed suddenly to surround her and draw in close to her. She heard a low whistle. She recognised it. It meant that all was well on the beach and that the beach boys controlled it.

She turned to Premasiri. 'I think I'll go back, I'll come another night. There is no moon. The turtle will not lay eggs on a moonless night like this.'

'But you will, missy. You'll lay,' she heard one of the men say.

She could not recognise the coarse voice or the

vulgar laugh that puked up the words. They crowded in on her. Someone spread an arm around her hips. She felt a hand creep in through the beach cloth to circle her breast. 'Like a ripe jumbu,' she heard a voice as close to her lips as it could get. Terrified, she writhed and shouted this name and that. But there was no reply. They held her by the arms and soon clamped shut her mouth, stifling her screams.

She was dragged towards the sea. They laid her down almost gently. The sea flooded close up and around her, and she struggled to push herself up but the sand was wet and formless in her grasp. The wind flung her cloth out and away from her like violent flapping wings. Still she struggled for release.

But then she sensed a voice that compelled silence. 'Don't be afraid,' it said to her from within a sudden hollow of stillness, 'I'm here, I'll be with you.'

Aruni sighed tiredly, and lifted her arms towards the voice. It continued insidiously to stroke away her terror. She began to crawl into it, into the voice, so gentle and soothing, all blanketing. Her rigid body began to melt, turning soft and pliant in the arms that held her down.

Did she begin to relax? Did she begin to feel

protected at last by those to whom she wanted so much to belong?

She gave up struggling. She couldn't recognise who it was that held her. But she nestled into the curve of his shoulder. She whispered, 'Please, please look after me.' Yes, he said, yes, nuzzling his face against her neck. She rested against him. She felt the fear drain away. She felt she was coming home. She felt she *was* home, on this wet sand, with this body up close against hers, and the intimately whispering voice. She was again gliding in the catamaran that windless night at sea, Premasiri telling her to abandon herself to it – so she'd know how it felt – like an embryo ensconced in the womb.

She began to feel his face with her fingers, softly, tenderly. Its strength, its sweat, its strange familiarity. She wondered if her mother had lain in such arms as this. Had awakened such desire. She felt him move against her and strained towards him. She heard him laugh then, a soft contemptuous laugh.

'She's ready, all wet and ready,' he said.

And then they raped her. Some she recognised, some she didn't. She lay inert, as if she hardly felt the repeated thrust to her most hurting depths.

She saw Premasiri's face in the line of men. She

felt his lips clamp down on hers. She felt her breasts sore, her body torn and stripped. She swallowed another scream and another. But like bile, they welled up and out of her, thick and bitter. Later, there were only cries, and whispers. And silences aching into the night. Aruni lay crucified, her arms flung out, her legs pressed close and painfully one against the other. They left her.

She must have lain there for hours. When she finally looked around, the sunrise was before her. A marigold sky: warm and orange. She watched it distantly. She thought of Paul and how they'd watch the dawn breaking. How he would whisper, 'Look, Aruni, like a woman stretching awake after a long, long and sensual night.' And how sometimes she would press into him as he read the Bible to her in the early morning hours. And talk to her of miracles. It all seemed so far away from her. The sunrise, Paul's voice, the love that he made so real in the promise of dawn. She saw the sky glisten with memories of those nights and dawns. But she lay disconnected. She could barely move. It seemed the sand had sucked her in where she lay, drop by pitiable drop, and that she belonged to it now.

At last, she staggered to her feet. She began to drag herself towards the sea. The beach cloth trailed in the sand behind her. Thoughts rose unbidden. These were her mother's relatives and friends. These, her people. She could not even begin to understand. Who they were, or who she was. The water swirled around her. She waded further in. A wave flung her to her knees, and she surrendered. It receded, carrying the cloth away. She stood up and watched. Soaked red, entangling seaweed, it curled and disappeared. Slowly, she turned towards the land.

Later that morning, the women discovered the cloth washed ashore. It was too soiled to sell even to the poor local folk. Just fit for those beach dogs which dragged around anything even faintly smelling of blood.

acknowledgements

The novel was assisted by an Individual Writer's Grant from the Literature Board of the Australia Council and a Project Completion Grant from the Faculty of Arts, Monash University.

Special thanks to all my family in Australia and Sri Lanka for their unshakable faith in my writing; Jennifer Strauss, Meg and Clive Probyn, and Makarand Paranjape for their presence in my writing life; Clare Forster, Ali Watts, Kay Ronai, Belinda Byrne, Nikki Townsend, Leanne Marcuzzi and Angela Crocombe of Penguin Australia for their wonderful attention to the book.

Finally, to my mother, Brenda Walaliyadde, who first led me to the songs of the sea; Samantha Abrew and Bill Ashcroft with whom I returned to them; and Sunil Ariyaratne, my lyrical inspiration – thank you.

Early extracts from the novel have been published in *Gas and Air: Tales of Pregnancy, Birth and Beyond*, ed. by Jill Dawson and Mago Daly (London: Bloomsbury, 2003), *Penguin Summer Stories 1* (2001), and *Options: Special 50th Anniversary Issue No 1*, ed. by Neloufer de Nel (Colombo: 1998).

From reviews of *If the moon smiled*:

If the moon smiled is a poignant, painful tale of personal cataclysms and traumas; a tortuous journey of adjustments, tensions and human relationships within an emigrant family.

The writer's lyrical imagery is breathtaking ... Lokugé's words dance and cry in her pages in a way that is reminiscent of Amit Chaudhuri's precise lyricism ... *If the moon smiled* is a brooding, moody, nostalgic and haunting success.

The Financial Review

... what a beautifully written, sad and touching story this is ... Lokugé writes with poise and a silk smooth touch.

Gauzy images ... unfurl as gently and lusciously as spring petals. As the mother of boys I love too fiercely, I found her exploration of the relationship between mother and son almost unbearably poignant.

The Weekend Australian

The enduring quality of the novel is its refined understanding and sensitive portrayal of intense emotion.

Canberra Sunday Times

Poignantly beautiful ...

The Advertiser

... *If the moon smiled* becomes a study of the pressure between generations as much as the friction of cultural demands.

The Australian Review of Books

The harsh psychological truths of this story are intertwined with Lokugé's use of the poetic language of Sri Lankan Buddhism. It movingly conveys the tragedy of the migrant generation their children's success stories leave behind.

The Bulletin

Chandani Lokugé's haunting elegy for a particular kind of unexamined life, is moving, unsettling and unfailingly attractive. The writing is consistently beautiful ...

The Sunday Times
(Sri Lanka)

Original in conception, subtly ambiguous in its exploration of Manthri's emotional vulnerability, Chandani Lokugé's novel is heartbreakingly true to the inner lives of many Sri Lankan women 'at home' and abroad.

The Book Review